I0659719

3 Under the Moon

MARCO SIENA

ENGLISH LANGUAGE TRANSLATION
by
MICHAEL R. HUDSON

RAVEN'S HEAD
PRESS

NEVER SAY NEVERMORE

NEVER SAY NEVERMORE

First Edition • January 2016 • Raven's Head Press • English Language
Copyright © 2016 Marco Siena and Michael R. Hudson • All rights
reserved.

Editor: Diana Nichols
Cover Design: Michael Hudson
.

PUBLISHERS NOTE

Raven's Head Press
Ravensheadpress.com
ISBN-13: 978-0692624678 • ISBN-10: 0692624678

I want to dedicate this book to my daughter, Eleonora Emilia, for giving my books compelling titles as well as challenging me to write stories that live up to those titles. It isn't always easy...

—Marco Siena

3 Under the Moon

MARCO SIENA

ENGLISH LANGUAGE TRANSLATION
by
MICHAEL R. HUDSON

YELLOW CAR AND SILVER BULLETS

CHAPTER ONE

Jerry hated, above all, one thing in life: to wait. He couldn't bear to wait without being in control, looking at the clock all the time. He remained closed up in that pub, continuing to order something, hoping that Schnitzel would show up. The man was a pain in the ass.

Passing cars splashed water up over the sidewalks, causing the few passers-by still outside their homes to curse, surprised by the sudden downpour.

He looked again at his watch and mobile phone. Finally Schnitzel's phone call came in.

He paid the bill and walked out quickly, covering his head with his jacket. He looked up and down the street but didn't see Schnitzel. A car slowly approached and the driver flashed the high beam as a signal to catch his attention. He ran toward it and recognized Schnitzel's huge bulk behind the wheel. He threw himself into the passenger seat and, without a word, gave a sign for Schnitzel to keep on going.

"You bought a yellow car," said Jerry.

"Yup. Nice, huh?" said the fat man. Jerry sighed. He lit a cigarette and wiped the condensation from his side window.

"You bought a fucking… yellow car. Are you, maybe, stoned?"

Schnitzel froze with his eyes dazed and his mouth locked in an O. "I don't understand, Jerry. You told me to buy a fast car and I did. Hell, you look comfortable enough. Look how soft and velvety the seats are? That's Alcantara, you know?"

Jerry was unimpressed. He stroked the seats, trying to find something good to say about the yellow ride but couldn't thing of anything. "I bet it's going to piss Cliff off."

In the small mind of Schnitzel, an army of tiny men was trying to connect the synapses quickly, to find a reason or something that would prove why Cliff would have, as it were, a negative reaction to the car. He knew that Cliff was not as patient and kind as Jerry, although he sounded less gruff than the latter.

A cold shiver ran down his spine, as he turned onto Tabard Street, splashing water on a couple of kids returning home from school.

"Listen to how the engine sings?" he ventured.

"Look, you can tell me that this thing can fly, but the fact that you spent almost eight thousand Sterling for a car that looks like a canary is going to send Cliff on a rampage. Our job is to follow a man, and you bring me a machine that flashes like a neon sign in a neighborhood of whores. Where's your brain man?"

The fat man reflected on the words of his friend and finally a glimmer of light entered his skull, lighting the way to more synaptic connections. The man who they had to follow was a real hell, according to Cliff, and Cliff knew a lot about devils. You could bet good money on the words of Cliff. He had called Jerry and Schnitzel in to help him follow the bastard on behalf of Madame Astrelle, who assured him the man was a werewolf, a real one, just like in the movies. Schnitzel really didn't believe it, although for two hundred thousand pounds he was willing to believe anything.

Cliff, however, was a real know-it-all in terms of the occult, monsters, and stuff like that. Hell, that's why the French girl had contacted him in the first place.

They arrived at the pub on Snowfields indicated by Cliff almost on time, despite Schnitzel's delay in picking up Jerry. Cliff was waiting for them inside the pub, drinking a dark beer that still held a head of white foam. When he saw them, he nodded his head.

"Our man?" whispered Jerry, sitting and looking around warily.

"I think he went to the bathroom. He's been sitting over there in the background all the time. Have you got a decent car this time?"

Jerry looked away, pretending to look for the waiter and leaving

Schnitzel in utter embarrassment and panic. The big man licked his lips but they seemed glued together. Finally he muttered, "Yeah, it's a beautiful car, Cliff. I guarantee it."

"Why am I suddenly uncomfortable with this? What have you done?"

"It was only four thousand Sterling."

Cliff blinked his eyelids nervously. "Only four thousand? Correct me if I'm wrong, but didn't you just buy one at fifteen and then turn around and resell at four after just one week's worth of use?"

The waiter came just in time, saving Schnitzel's ass for the moment. They ordered two dark beers and a couple of sandwiches.

"Look, Cliff, we'll get rid of it tomorrow and swap it for something better, alright? This time I'll handle it," said Jerry in a condescending tone as he eyed his fat partner.

Cliff leaned on the table, sipped his beer and wiped the foam from his mustache with a napkin. "Is there something I'm missing? Why are you now in such a hurry to get rid of it?"

Jerry clenched his teeth, realizing the gaffe he had just made. He had failed to follow the dialogue and had not noticed that Schnitzel had not mentioned the color of the fireball.

"We'll explain later. Someone just came out of the toilet," whispered Schnitzel. His attempt to be professional, like a secret agent, ended in a tragicomic manner.

The guy who had just left the restroom was tall with long curly black hair collected in the back into a short ponytail. He was carrying a black leather bag, slightly discolored, close to his side. He sat down at a table in the back, where a half glass of dark liquor awaited him. As if nothing had happened, he threw the drink down in one gulp.

"Did you see his hands?" Cliff asked softly.

Jerry tried to look out of the corner of his eye, while Schnitzel, making wise, nodded an affirmative to Cliff. Jerry didn't notice anything strange about the man, embarrassed that his idiot partner had noticed something before him.

"No, Cliff. What thing?" asked Jerry.

"You tell him, Dumpling," said Cliff sarcastically.

11

"It's Schnitzel."

"All right... Schnitzel. Couldn't you find a decent fake name? Something that fits you better instead of a lean cut of beef for a moniker?"

Schnitzel shrugged apologetically.

"So, tell me what is it about his hands?" Jerry asked impatiently.

"Something tells me neither one of you guys understand shit. So I'll tell you, dear Jerry. He's wearing gloves," said Cliff.

"Gloves? So what? I wear them too. It's cold outside. It's only three or four degrees above freezing outside, " said Schnitzel.

Cliff shook his head sadly. "Don't you guys ever learn anything? He's wearing fingerless gloves. He never takes them off. It's needless to ask you why, so I'll just explain for you two numbskulls. Is he still sitting?"

"Yes," replied Jerry and Schnitzel in unison.

"Werewolves have recognizable signs on their palms that can be easily picked up by a keen eye. By someone as experienced as me." Cliff's tone warned Jerry and Schnitzel that they could be in for the man's typical arrogant scholarly dissertation that could last for over an hour, in his efforts to seek confirmation through his high-sounding words and bombastic attitude. It seems Cliff was always eager to enchant the minds of people like Jerry and Schnitzel. Even his green eyes, happy and bright, revealed the pride and confidence he took in impressing his two stupid accomplices with his obvious vast knowledge of culture.

"What are these signs?" asked Jerry. He knew that Cliff had expected his question, from that smug feline look on his face.

"Well, you start by setting set up a small handbook on how to recognize the creatures of *darkness*." He said 'darkness' with a certain solemnity and emphasis.

"What handbook?" asked Schnitzel. "Cliff, try not making this too complicated, huh?" That statement made Cliff's chest swell even more.

"All right Schnitzel, forget the handbook. I'll explain later. Let's go back to that damn werewolf sitting back there. As you can see he's comfortable there as if nothing had happened, but, I assure you, he's ready to tear the first victim who crosses his path when he is hungry."

At that moment the waiter came and stopped upon hearing the word hungry. "Are you hungry sir? Can I get you anything?"

"No, no. Shit, you just ruined the mood," said Cliff gesturing the waiter away with a wave of his hand.

The waiter frowned and left with a shrug and Cliff continued, "The *lupus hominarius* usually have a pentacle in the palm, of at least one of their hands, even though it may be covered by coarse growth of hair. It would be embarrassing to go around with bare hands like that, don't you agree?"

Schnitzel looked at his hands, trying to imagine them covered with fur inside. He pursed his mouth in disgust. "And then what?" he asked, now fascinated by Cliff's words.

"Eyebrows. See how thick and are united they are above the nose?"

Jerry turned around, pretending to look around for the waiter. Schnitzel narrowed his eyes to see better. The man's eyebrows actually looked like a single black line above the darkened eyes. While they could not see the black of his pupils, they could see that the man had a look of fierceness about his countenance.

"Damn..." whispered Schnitzel incredulously. He was almost starting to believe the words of Cliff, and that the French were not all crazy. He swallowed.

"And the neck? Notice anything strange?"

Then Jerry stood up. "What the fuck, I can't see any of this stuff you're blabbering about from here."

"Where the hell are you going? Idiot!" said Cliff trying to stop him.

Jerry walked over to the man who at that time was jotting something in a pocket notebook. On a plate before him was a T-bone steak, eaten entirely except for the fat, yellow and greasy. Next to the plate stood a bottle of Italian red that looked empty, as did the glass of liquor they'd seen him gulp down earlier.

"Excuse me, are you by any chance...?"

The man looked up at him. Those damn brooding black eyes did not have much shine in them. The man had a musky smell, far from unpleasant, almost hypnotic, very masculine.

"Who?" the man asked. His voice was deep and low, almost a growl.

"Sammy. You're not Sammy?"

"No."

"Okay, I'm sorry. Sammy was in college with me ... time does—"

"I'm not Sammy."

"I'm sorry to have bothered you. Have a nice day."

Satisfied, Jerry returned to the table, dropping heavily back into his chair. He grabbed his glass and drank the last drop of beer.

"I thought, honestly, that the idiot in this bunch was Schnitzel, but even he's not that damn stupid. Are you off your rocker?" said Cliff.

Schnitzel tried to figure out if he had just been given a compliment or if he had been insulted, and concluded that either was better than what Jerry just got from Cliff. He motioned to the waiter to order something, just to celebrate.

"You asked about the neck and I saw it," said Jerry. "He bought the song and dance I sold him. No one is better than me when it comes to putting on a charade like that. I'm like one of those illusionists, you know? I'll focus on one point and the target won't care. They haven't a clue!"

"Yeah, for sure. So, what did you see? Schnitzel here is quivering with curiosity to know," sneered Cliff.

Jerry settled himself on the wooden chair, which was becoming uncomfortable. He couldn't stand chairs without padding. The wallet in his back pocket was starting to bother him, as well as the house keys stored in the other.

"He has a leather pouch around his neck, with a black tie."

"A leather bag? What kind?"

"Like ... like a pasty bag."

The waiter arrived just then. "Do you want some fresh pasties?"

"No, no pasties. Bring us two beers… no, make it three," replied Jerry annoyed.

Again, the waiter shrugged and walked away, shaking his head, jotting down the order in his notebook.

"But I would have eaten the pasties," said Schnitzel.

"Screw you and the pasties. Drink your beer and be ready. We're not playing. That bag around his neck is his fetish," explained Cliff.

This new statement threw his two accomplices into even more of a panic, causing them to think that the bag around the man's neck could evoke some kind of terrible and cruel demons from the underworld. Schnitzel, and he did not know why, also linked the word 'fetish' to something sexual and felt an uncontrollable itch in his backside, imagining sodomites with horns and tails ready to let him know the limits and capacity of his rectum before his sphincter gave out.

"Ouch," he said thoughtfully.

"Well, now we both know what you *think* a fetish means. But I don't believe you know what it really means in this instance," said Jerry smugly.

The fat man proved with his dullard gaze that he didn't understand anything.

Cliff grinned at the two and said, "Okay, let me explain to you two cocks what a fetish is. Inside that bag, definitely made of human skin, lies the power of the wolf. It contains a mysterious mixture of herbs, animal and human hair, and a small piece of engraved wood, lowercase and of unknown language, that defines the formula of metamorphosis! It is said the bag even contains a drop of amber cypress in which are imprisoned the rays of the moon."

Jerry pulled on his lip thoughtfully. The man had to be a jerk, no doubt, but think of a bag in which was contained everything that Cliff had just said. It seemed highly unlikely. Looking around he saw cell phones, TV screens, electric lights and cars, how can you believe in magic and witchcraft? No, it could not be true. Maybe the man was mentally ill, convinced that he could change into animals. People like Cliff did nothing but give him more rope allowing him to become even more convinced of its power. But Jerry was too much of a pragmatic to be able to fall for such crap. He believed only in what was visible in front of him, and now that man over there walked on two legs and drank wine.

"I think I'm going to shit in my pants, Cliff," said Schnitzel. He clutched his hand on the beer glass so hard that Cliff was afraid it would explode into a thousand pieces under the fat man's grip.

"Squeeze your legs together, big boy. We've got to move," said Jerry.

Their target had risen. He approached the counter in a calm and relaxed manner, paid and left.

It had finally stopped raining outside. Jerry thanked the Lord for this grant. Sitting in the car with his fat partner about to burst behind the steering wheel, facing the prospect of driving on wet roads were not covered in his list of enjoyable hobbies. For just a moment his mind drifted to the pension plan he so desired and hoped to enjoy as soon as possible and how it would be filled with days of sitting on the shore of a pond watching the float of a fishing rod in his hands.

They waited twenty seconds, checking their watches and then rose together. Almost. Schnitzel was a moment behind them.

CHAPTER TWO

If the rain had stopped, the cold did not want to. It was penetrating damp and treacherous right through the collars of their jackets that, although heavy, could not keep it out.

Cliff looked around; waiting for his friends to show him the car Schnitzel had bought. It had to be, at least, an almost new German sedan to have cost so much money. He could not believe his eyes when they walked over to the yellow car.

"What the fuck are you doing? We don't have time for you two to be clowning around. Now where's the car?"

Jerry looked at Schnitzel fearing the mess that was about to burst.

"This is it, Chief."

"Chief... shit! I told you to call me Cliff. Don't call me Chief. You got that?"

"Okay, I'm sorry," replied Schnitzel meekly.

"Jerry, at least tell me this thing's a joke. You couldn't have bought a lemon instead of a real car, because that's what this damn thing looks like! How are you going to go unnoticed with this yellow piece of shit?"

Failing to argue and in finding a decent excuse, they got into the car with the reproaches of Cliff resounding in their ears. By the time they had fastened their seat belts, the target had driven past them in a black sport car, heading out onto Weston Street.

Schnitzel started the car, gunning the accelerator as he did, hoping the powerful roar of the yellow fireball would get a positive remark from Cliff. In response, he earned a slap on the back of the head.

"Instead of acting like an idiot and attracting even more attention, just follow the damn car before we lose it!" scolded Cliff.

"Okay, Cliff, sorry. However, with that old jalopy he's sure to lose us," justified the fat man behind the wheel.

Cliff looked up at the sky in despair. "That's why I don't want you picking our cars. You don't know shit! The target's car is a seventy-nine. If I'm right it's held together better than your brain, and could probably squeeze off a hundred and twenty mph smoothly while you're still here in this coffee maker muttering to yourself. Now hurry up!"

The black car was actually distancing them. The driver, their target, drove with the agility of a snake through the traffic on Weston. Several times, Schnitzel, in an effort not to lose him, risked rearranging the sides of the other vehicles that separated the two vehicles. He earned a series of unflattering insults from a guy driving a van, who promised to run over his ass if he didn't slow down. On any other occasion Schnitzel would have obeyed the van driver's command, but the hard look that Cliff gave him made him realize that they were on a job and could not afford to lose their target.

"Look, he turned south," said Jerry.

"Yeah, but where is he going?" Schnitzel asked to no one in particular.

"You just follow him and we'll find out," said Cliff.

After more than an hour, the black sports car turned left, heading onto a side street that placed them less than thirty miles from the coast. A sign indicated that they were ten miles outside of Brighton. The road intersected with another smaller road that was little more than a joke. It gave the impression that they were driving straight on the heath rather than a real road.

"Stop here. We can't continue," said Cliff.

"Why not?" Schnitzel asked.

Again Cliff wondered whether to keep after the target or to stop now, before all his work blew up in smoke. "Do you see any more cars on the road other than us?"

"So?" insisted Schnitzel.

"Then, you idiot, a yellow car like this on an empty road would arouse some suspicion, right?" interjected Jerry. "Provided that the target hasn't already noticed that he was being followed."

"Turn off the lights. We'll wait for a minute or two and then we'll go," said Cliff.

"And if we lose our way?"

"Not going to happen. I'll be warming my hands over a fire where we'll pass the night somewhere down there, where there are lights," said Cliff.

They opened their eyes to see better in the dark, trying to penetrate the veil of fog that had descended on the heath. Shortly thereafter it would become dense to the point of even preventing bearings. They saw in the distance a few feeble lights coming from the homes of a small village. A beautiful rural village of shepherds was just what it took to make them anonymous, that and their beautiful yellow car.

"You go on ahead on foot," declared Cliff suddenly.

Jerry and Schnitzel looked at each other, in the dim light of the passenger compartment, for mutual aid, failing miserably and finding only confusion ... and fear.

"No, Cliff, fuck. We just talked about monsters, and now you want us to walk in the dark of the countryside, without you, in the fog and frost, "Jerry protested, shivering.

"Schnitzel?" asked Cliff.

"I'm with Jerry. I've got a fear of the devil, I admit, and I've got to take a shit so bad I can't stand it. I'd never make it there, if we are going to have to walk it."

Cliff sighed, and felt in his pockets to check if everything was in order. "Come on, come on, move your ass. You expressed your opinion, and now we move."

Jerry, confused, looked at his fat partner who was clenching his teeth and quivering, perhaps because of the cold, or perhaps to retain his pressing bowel needs. " C'mon Cliff, we can just take the car."

"I have to take a dump... right now!" squealed Schnitzel.

"I'm not going to repeat myself again. You two got the yellow fucking car and now we are paying the price for your stupidity. Remember that I also have to tramp through this bloody cold fog on foot because of you when I could be nice and warm with a brandy in front of me. Now come on, hurry up."

They got out of the car and the freezing cold turned their breath into wispy tendrils. Jerry picked up his bag and checked the safety on the revolver he was carrying. He wondered silently if werewolves really required silver bullets. He knew that Cliff had some made by a guy called John the Deaf, down in the East End. He was tempted to ask him for at least one because, from what was said, only weapons made of silver could kill a werewolf, whether it was true or not. In all other cases everything tried would fail to kill one of the monsters.

Schnitzel went to get something from the trunk but suddenly stopped, feeling yet another sharp spasm in his belly. He wasn't going to make it much longer.

"Look sorry ass, just go over there behind that mound and do your business. Who's going to see? Are you really that shy? Or are you afraid that a goblin's going to take a big bite out of your ass?" said Cliff impatiently.

"And what if the wolf comes out and attacks me? He's a lot scarier than a goblin!"

"What… He's down there in the village, he's not going to teleport up here to detach your balls."

Despite the urgency, Schnitzel was reluctant, and shifted his weight from one leg to another to help him hold his bowels in place.

"Shit, go where you said Cliff, pig world! You'll miss the guy, and then you will be pain. "

"I have an idea. You know that werewolves are somehow controlled by fate?" asked Cliff.

They both shook their heads. "What?" Schnitzel asked.

"I will explain shortly. One evening a thousand years ago, two brothers had to cross the Barnes North Yorkshire bridge. In those days news had spread that a tribe of werewolves lived around there. As was the custom, the brothers decided to cast lots to see who would die and who would be spared a mauling, trusting in fate. It seems that those whose coin had landed on the cross all shared the same unfortunate fate."

Jerry lit a cigarette with an automatic gesture, listening intently to the conversation. Schnitzel forgot about his bowels for a moment as he listened closely to Cliff's story. "And then?" He asked with a small voice.

"Well, the two brothers threw the coin and both left to cross the bridge, the older brother losing and having to go first. He turned to the power of fate and went out into the night, urging his horses ever faster as he neared the bridge. Suddenly four werewolves came out of nowhere, utterly destroying the mounts. But, and here comes the fun part, when they reached the elder brother he bowed his head in surrender and they let him go, tearing apart only the two who had crossed first and… that just happened to be the two… horses."

The two listeners were petrified, motionless as they thought about the image of the cross on the brothers' coin when it finally landed. Schnitzel wished as never before in his life to see the face of the Queen on the opposite side of that old coin, and he imagined her winking back at him.

"Okay, we'll flip a coin," suggested Jerry.

Schnitzel rummaged around in his pockets, and found a brand new Sterling. He tossed it up in the air and didn't wait, even a second, to look at the result. Attempting the beat out fate, he took careful refuge behind the mound. Fortunately for him the Queen had blessed him. Relieved and already behind the hill, he started to undo his belt and drop his pants.

"Oh dear God! I'll have to cross the heath alone! I'll die," whined Jerry. "Help me Cliff!"

Cliff chuckled, snatching the cigarette from Jerry's hand and taking a deep drag. "It was a lie my friend. At least this time it was. If I had not invented this story, the fat boy would literally have shit all over himself right here in front of us."

"What if Schnitzel would not have been so lucky?"

"I figure it was a fifty percent chance that wouldn't happen. Right?"

They crossed the misty heath, cold and in silence, their fogged breath the only signs of their presence. Schnitzel was wheezing with every step he took. They turned constantly at every little noise, wincing when they came upon the barking of a dog. No one dared to speak.

Jerry shone his small flashlight that hooked on to a key ring at a signpost that read: PLUMPTON Population 300

"Plumpton?" read Jerry.

"Yup, Plumpton," confirmed Cliff. "What's the matter?"

"I don't know. I guess I expected something more somber, like Slaughterton or some place similar. Instead we end up in this village with a last known count of three hundred souls. Not bad, Huh?"

Schnitzel, now feeling complete relief from his misery, urged his partners to continue. "Come on guys, come on, it's so cold out here!"

The main road, crossing the area from west to east, was barely wide enough for a van to pass, in case you ever have to go there. It was not even paved, and it still retained the cobblestones typical of the Roman era. To make it even more dismal the area lacked any kind of lighting. The only lamps were those they passed hanging outside the doors. Jerry found himself thinking that those lights gave the countryside the look and feel of a cemetery, more than that of an English country village.

The three men looked around, casting furtive glances down a few streets that opened into other small streets that seemingly led nowhere. They were lost in the dark, and concluded that in reality everything was there, close to the old Roman road.

Finally they saw a small sign of civilization. It came in the form of a sign that swung back and forth in the wind just above the front door of a cheerfully lit pub. Again Jerry was expecting something like *The Slaughtered Ox*, and was amazed to see that it read *The Silly Duck*, engraved in wood. They spotted the black tail of their target's car sticking out of an alley next to the pub.

"He's in here," said Cliff.

"What the hell, are we following a drunk doing some kind of pub crawl, or a werewolf with a drinking problem?" asked Jerry, trying to be ironic.

Neither Cliff nor Schnitzel laughed or made comments.

Looking inside the window, as opposed to what they had expected, there sat a number of fat and jovial guests. There were sounds of laughter, as well as a few catcalls, most likely directed at the winsome waitress. Certainly their target was not tearing anyone apart… yet.

"What do we do, Chief?" asked Schnitzel. He looked around like a terrified child. It created a very paradoxical scene. If someone had been paying attention he would have scratched his head in disbelief because the only one who looked scared was the big man, Schnitzel, who was at least six and a half feet tall with shoulders the envy of a bear.

"Chief, my ass. Don't call me Chief, I told you."

"Sorry. What do we do?"

Cliff scratched his beard, finding it wet from the fog. He felt they were in a dilemma as to whether they had really attracted the attention of man in the London pub, or rather, had Jerry done so by drawing the man out with that stupid question. Now all he wanted was to find a way to observe the movements of the man without arousing his suspicion. Being right there in that country pub after being seen by him in London earlier might smell a bit funny to their target. Only Schnitzel would not understand.

"Let me ask you. While we're still waiting, would you rather still be outside freezing in the field or, alternatively, would you rather we enter and enjoy a nice shot. Or two," said Cliff finally.

"Oh, I already know. You want me to say in the field!" said Schnitzel, spreading his arms and shaking his head in disgust.

Cliff glared at him and pointed his finger. "Shut your mouth, you jinx! We're going inside!"

Jerry looked at his two partners, in turn, with a look of reproach; he lit a cigarette and was ready to get inside the place to warm up. The laughter and the cheerful light coming under the door and through the windows gave him a sense of warmth and well being even though he was about to again meet up with a real caring type in the purported werewolf, the one with the pasty bag around his neck and the hairy hands.

Cliff put his cell phone in his pocket, after a brief conversation in which he had explained where they were, and all the details that had brought them to decide whether to enter or not, including the brilliant idea that maybe Jerry had compromised their coverage.

"What did she say?" asked Jerry anxious.

"Beyond that you're an idiot?"

Jerry curled his lip. "Yup."

"She said for us to go in and act like we don't give a damn. We can't risk that our target takes a back window and gets out. He may actually have noticed us before now, thanks also to that beautiful yellow car you bought, Schnitzel."

"Thanks Cliff."

"That was *not* an appreciation."

"Oh."

"Madame Astrelle says that our target is smarter than us and if we can imagine that, thanks to his supernatural senses, he might have already have smelled our scent and recognized us from that."

Jerry felt somewhat relieved. He could freely enter and warm up a bit. In addition he would feel safer inside the room in the midst of people, rather than out in the cold, standing in the middle of that damn fog.

Cliff took the initiative and opened the door wide. It was not what he expected. It was a traditional old stone pub with candles instead of electric lights, a cozy and warm room with dark wood, well kept and it was currently hosting at least fifty people. He had also envisioned that when they opened the door, everyone would be silenced, staring at them with grim looks. But the patrons paid no attention, except for a pretty maid with reddish hair and full cheeks, who came to meet them with a smile on her face.

"Good evening gentlemen. Just the three?"

They looked at each other amazed, including Cliff. "Yes, just the three of us, thank you."

"Well, follow me. I have a table reserved for guests."

In the 'table reserved for guests' there was something ambiguous in her wording, at least according to Jerry, who gradually realized he was moving move and more towards Schnitzel's wavelength. And he did not like that one bit. "Reserved for guests?" he asked. It had come out of his mouth without thinking.

The waitress smiled and showed them the round table in the back. "It's a table reserved for new customers, to keep them away from the loud noise that comes from our regular customers, such as Messrs.' Jenkins and Gray. It can be a bit confusing. We do not want people to be disturbed by their shouts and songs, or their dirty jokes. They're sheep farmers, so have patience."

The kind and outspoken girl made them relax, transporting them in a country where anything could happen, except for them being able to hear a dirty joke or a ribald song from a bunch of sheep farmers.

There was a smell of moss nearby. Jerry turned out of instinct and saw their target sitting at a table only a few feet from them. He was eating something with a hearty appetite, drinking at intervals from a wooden cup. He seemed not to notice them.

"Here," she whispered.

Cliff turned to Schnitzel and tried to hide behind him. "Look at how the guy eats, the pig. At least it seems that he also likes normal food."

"But it is not normal food," she whispered to Schnitzel.

"Oh, no? What is it then?" he asked.

"Haggis!"

"That Scottish shit! Oh no, I'm going to be sick!" moaned Schnitzel.

Jerry gave him a slap on the back. "Go easy jerk. You know that my grandmother was Scottish, right?"

Cliff made a gesture with his hands to keep them quiet. "Keep your cool, we do not want to attract additional attention from this guy. We eat and drink as if nothing has happened."

Around midnight, the place turned into an indoor village festival, with songs in an old dialect, jokes and plenty of beer flowing, moving from table to table. Who they had been up until the time they'd entered the pub didn't seem to matter and the three were continually plied with free rounds on the house. Jerry and Schnitzel were not men of willpower and had already swallowed at least a gallon of beer each. Cliff, by contrast, remained sober, smoking his hand-rolled cigarettes, after asking permission from Chloe, the friendly waitress.

Their target, however, remained impassive, as if he were not even in the room, writing down notes in that mysterious notebook, rummaging and stroking his fingers over the bag that hung about his neck and, in some cases, checking the time on an old-fashioned pocket watch that was held by a chain within his coat. Jerry mimicked him, making the gesture of holding a monocle over one eye and miming to consult a pocket watch.

Mr. Jenkins had just stood up on a table to make an

announcement, when a man entered, all bundled up, and everyone said goodbye, breaking for a moment the jovial atmosphere that had been created. The newcomer went to sit in front of their target and finally Jenkins could finish what he had started.

Cliff and his companions became quickly silent, however, all ears in trying to obtain at least part of the conversation between the newcomer and their man. However, every attempt was in vain because of the noise that Jenkins had created. Everyone was laughing once again, cackling drunk and singing a song about the head of a bandit that was rolling down a hill.

When the man got up to leave, the alleged werewolf sat still for a moment and Cliff was able to read his lips as he said to his departing companion, 'in half an hour'. The rendezvous place he was, unfortunately, unable to grasp.

"Now all we have to do is wait for him to leave and follow him. This time we close the accounts," said Cliff.

"It's not because Madame Astrelle is angry though, right?" asked Schnitzel.

Cliff snorted. He could not bear to have someone above him when it came to action. He preferred to have carte blanche. So he called the woman. The conversation only lasted a few moments. The line was broken.

"Madame Astrelle told us to move and follow our target. We absolutely have to find out why he came here, and to se if we can find out exactly who he is. Are you guys now seeing that I was right?"

The fat man smirked. "You're always right, Chief!"

"Stop calling me Chief!"

"But why?"

"Because if the enemy identifies who the boss is, that's going to be his first target."

CHAPTER THREE

The man walked with a slow pace down the cobblestone street. The only noise the three men heard was that of his boot heels clicking on the stones. He didn't take the car, having left it in the alley next to the pub. Jerry had rated the vehicle at over twenty-five thousand pounds, saying that his cousin Ralph, a restorer of old cars, had arranged a sale on one like it last year, selling it for no less than twenty thousand.

"But it's French made and that makes it a piece of shit. Look, it even drives on the wrong side. Who the fuck wants to waste all that money," protested Schnitzel.

"Oh, so now you know all about driving? Don't you know that this is the same car that the French president drives?"

"Ah, you're exaggerating! If it was the president's car then why has that guy got it now? And how do you even know that it was the president's car anyway?"

Jerry paused, looking deep into Schnitzel's eyes. He shook his head. "I give up with you. I don't think you can be helped."

Cliff yanked them both back, causing them to flatten against the wall. "Be quiet you two and careful, dammit! He stopped and you didn't even notice!"

Their target was in front of a wooden barn, located at the bottom of the street, next to a small church. Jerry, in its place, would have expected to find the office of the municipality or the postal service, however the village focal point was just an... old barn.

"Well, I knew it, there's a church in the middle of all this," whined Schnitzel.

"That's enough. Let's get to the point. We need to find out what that devil is trying, and then break him down and get him to Madame Astrelle Pellacchia," said Cliff. He pulled the gun from his holster and automatically checked that it was loaded. Jerry caught a glimpse of one of the notorious silver bullets as it flashed for a second, and then disappeared back into Cliff's pocket.

Swallowing hard, he checked his revolver, feeling unarmed,

having only the standard issue bullets. Schnitzel, however, conjured up a sawed-off shotgun from inside his jacket, shivering, his teeth chattering when he opened the zipper.

"Look, Cliff, isn't that...?"

"What, dear Jerry?"

"...If I could just have one of those silver bullets?"

"Sure," said Cliff.

Jerry smiled and reached out.

"What is it?" said Cliff.

"The bullets..."

"I said that you could have one, but not mine, stupid. Go to Deaf and take care of your business like you do with a car. The important thing to keep in mind is that these are not the correct bullets for your cannon. These are for an automatic but you, Jerry, have a revolver."

Jerry felt his knees shake. Cliff's initial response had given hope to feel less helpless. Now there was the risk of being eaten. He wiped the cold sweat from his brow and blew on his fingers to warm them.

"Shall we?" asked Schnitzel anxiously.

"What is this sudden courage?"

"Our coin toss... I came out heads first, right? The wolf can't do anything to me," he said nonchalantly as he took off running toward the barn.

Jerry opened his eyes, holding back a scream, or rather a curse that would have rocked the small bell tower of the church. Cliff meanwhile seriously considered shooting the moron. Thank God the man had disappeared into the barn before noticing the big man that ran in his direction. He closed the door behind him with a crunch of wood and creaking hinges that needed oiling.

The others reached Schnitzel who had stopped in front of the barn, hands at his sides, gun pointed to the ground. The first thing Cliff did was to give him a kick in the ass.

"Nice move, troglodyte. What if he would have seen you?"

Schnitzel scratched his neck, fiddling with his toe in the gaps of paving stones. He looked like a child scolded by his father. A decidedly outsized baby.

"Okay guys, now the going gets tough. We go in preparing for the worst. Do not approach him. Aim for, if it's at all possible, the bag around his neck. If he's in human form the brain. If he's in the form of wolf try to keep my ass safe and away from its fangs. In any case, I'll finish it with silver once he's shot down. Okay?"

The plan Cliff laid out was clear: he would stay back, while they were trying to shoot it down without being eaten. Once that was done, Cliff would intervene with his precious silver bullets. Jerry seemed to think it was a shitty idea but he kept his mouth closed. Schnitzel, instead, was as charged as his shotgun. It was then that he flung open the door of the barn.

CHAPTER FOUR

Schnitzel took a step inside the barn, his number twelve feet encased within a pair of beige hiking boots, raising a puff of dust. Straw covered the floor of beaten earth, hard and icy. The three believed, in reality, it was just a barn, but they were surprised to see that the right side contained a row of horse stalls. A wide-eyed bay stuck its head out of one of the stalls, perhaps surprised to see a bear with human features crashing into its barn.

Someone had lit the metal lamps that hung from the central beam, illuminating the upper portion of the loft. That someone was their target, and as if nothing had happened, he was plotting something on the ground, using a kind of stick.

Schnitzel, shotgun at the ready and looking tough, motioned to the others to come in, feeling safe for the fact that he held the man at gunpoint.

"Hello," said the latter, without turning around.

He kept track of the squiggles he was drawing in the straw and dust, as quiet as a host that was setting the table for three newly arrived customers.

Schnitzel looked over to Cliff and Jerry, who shrugged simultaneously. "Hey, what... what are you doing?" he asked the target.

The man paused, and booted a tuft of hair that had fallen from his face. For the first time he looked at them, causing a chill to run through all three.

"I'm drawing a circle, can't you see?" He answered as if the answer was obvious.

"A circle? For what?" asked Schnitzel.

Cliff ran a hand over his beard, finding a crumb of bread stuck inside. He removed it and threw it to the ground in disgust. "He's definitely drawing a magic circle." He said this with an air of superiority.

The man laughed, a throaty sound without humor. "Clifford Sweetland, it is a pleasure to note that your erudition of the occult has quite improved."

"Chief, is your name really Clifford Sweetland?" asked Schnitzel.

"Shit, do not call me Chief!" yelled Cliff.

Jerry instinctively looked behind him, to make sure they were not being observed. All they needed was Cliff's yell to attract few curious drunks their way. Strangely enough, he saw nothing. He opened the door a crack and decided to watch.

"Well, now Clifford, I know that you're the boss," said the man.

Schnitzel put his big hand over his mouth, muttering his apologies to Cliff who stared back with glaring eyes. They saw that the man had begun to make marks in the dirt again. When Cliff noticed it, he took a step backward, gripping his gun firmly. Schnitzel gasped at his partner's sudden movement and jumped back, raising his rifle resting into the crook of his shoulder.

"Stop drawing ... that thing ... right now! It won't help save you from our bullets, man. This beauty will make a hole in you from side to side that you can see through!" said Schnitzel.

The man did not flinch. He drew two more signs, straightened and brushed his coat off with his hands, putting the stick under his arm. "I do not need this to protect me, but to protect you."

Cliff looked at Schnitzel who stared back. Both exhibited wide staring eyes like that of a boiled fish. Either of them would have been the envy of any drunkard at the local pub. If Schnitzel sought Cliff's support, this would certainly be the time for him to give it. Cliff tried to step back and examine the situation. He had to take up the reins. He decided to try and flaunt safety by folding his arms together and tilting his head to the side, posing like a slum tough.

"And you think we feel safe protected by that pile of squiggles?"

"But isn't it a magic circle?" asked Schnitzel.

"Shut up" whispered Cliff.

Once again their man moved slowly, seeming almost unaware and uncaring about the weapons and the alleged threats that Cliff wanted to convey.

"I would say that before long you will find out," he replied looking towards the doorway.

Jerry, who had a hand resting on the door, that was suddenly no longer there, became unbalanced and fell to the ground, swearing to a couple of guests of Paradise. When he looked up, he saw two naked men standing there in its place. They had gotten out of a white SUV parked a few steps from the church, almost hidden by the fog.

"And these naked freaks, who the hell are they?" Schnitzel asked. Without realizing it he had backed up and bumped into their man. Touching him, he felt a consistency as hard as wood and realized that the man was as tall as him, if not more so. Undoubtedly, however, he was not as heavy and bulky in stature. This consideration heartened him for a moment.

"Hey, you! What do we do with those two snakes outside?" asked Cliff, drawing a quick laugh out of Schnitzel and Jerry, who by then had gotten back up.

"They seem more like worms than snakes," added Schnitzel, mimicking a measurement between his thumb and index finger.

Cliff and Jerry laughed. The two men did not laugh. Neither did their target.

The biggest surprise, however, was when a naked woman came through the door casually, without giving any sign of feeling cold. Jerry gave a whistle of appreciation, as he ogled her toned and well shaped body.

"Madame Astrelle? Wha… what are you doing here?" asked Cliff.

Jerry looked at Schnitzel knowingly and nodded a sign of assent, pleased that he knew who the woman was. But what was she doing there naked in this weather? Even though it was screwed up, however, she remained a large piece of... The stern gaze of the woman froze that thought, forcing him to look away.

"Cliff," said Madame Astrelle. "You did a good job. Thank you."

"I'm glad to hear that," he replied sweetly, throwing a look of defiance to the man behind him.

"Madame Astrelle. But what a surprise. I thought it was the puppy of Jamaine who would follow me, and instead it's you. Women cannot do without me, obviously," said the man.

The woman snorted in derision. "And you, Juan have became increasingly arrogant."

"Coming from you that is a compliment."

He had taken a step forward without either Cliff or Schnitzel knowing it. He had crept between them like a shadow.

"Look after the lady," ventured Cliff to his companions.

"Ssstt," said Juan, putting a finger to his mouth. "Now you kids go away, because it's time for us to play. Okay?"

Schnitzel lost the light of reason and raised his shotgun, firing at the man's back. While Cliff seemed frightened, he fired in turn, once, twice, sending his silver bullets into the lungs of Juan, who fell heavily forward.

Schnitzel ran to Cliff and Jerry giggling hysterically, between terror and exhilaration, flaring heat and full of adrenaline.

"The wolf...?" he asked.

"He's dead," added Cliff. Nudging the fallen man, he added, "Stay down, mutt."

"He wasn't such a big deal great," said Jerry approaching. Madame Astrelle and her men stood still. They were not laughing. Something strange was happening with them. Their nostrils flared, as if they were filling their lungs with air. In fact, they were enjoying the smell of blood.

Before Cliff and his companions had realized it, the two naked men had thrown themselves to the ground, landing on their arms. Their bodies began to fill up with bumps, the skin splitting open in several places. Through the lacerations, irregular patches of dark red, gray, and black hairs came, bristly and shiny with blood. In the next instant, Cliff unfortunately realized what was happening, recognizing the ugly faces of the werewolf he had seen in comic books growing up. It seems that is where he had learned all the crap he had sold around the world, pretending to be an expert in the occult. This time his false curriculum would cost him his skin. But he did know a few tricks, and for security against just that, he rushed into the circle drawn by Juan.

"O Lord God of Heaven. What are these ugly things?" asked Schnitzel.

Jerry shouted something and tried to run for the exit. Unfortunately he was stopped by one of the beings that, until recently, had been one of the naked men. Fangs and claws tore at his back, after having torn open his throat from which now came a pitiful gurgling sound.

"What the hell," shouted Cliff. "Meatball, shoot him! What are you waiting for?"

Schnitzel fired but his aim was off, having just grazed one of the werewolves who were now approaching him. Their countenances had undergone a strange flicker when he fired, confusing his aim. Wasting no time, he threw himself backward landing inside the circle, thanking the deceased Juan who had drawn it so wide.

The werewolves snarled and circled, not daring to step into the ring.

"Stand back! I warn you that I have silver bullets in here!" screamed Cliff showing them the gun.

"Silver? You have been cheated, you fool," said Juan, rising up.

Schnitzel made the sign of the cross, kissed the Madonna at his throat, and began to pray. "There are no zombos, no zom—"

"Zombie, no zombies," corrected Cliff.

The two werewolves turned to Juan, standing up on their hind legs. Standing, they were almost as tall as him. Standing, they seemed to become more humanoid.

"And now, you can dance," Juan said, jumping to his feet, pulling two knives from out of his coat. The blades did not shine and did not reflect the light. They seemed to be made of darkness.

The werewolves attacked together. The horse whinnied and began to kick in its stall. The air became full of flying dust and straw, making Schnitzel sneeze and, in turn, fire off a couple of shotgun blasts in random directions. In the commotion, Cliff bent close to the ground, firing at random and hoping to hit something. Anything. He did not understand why, but in his mind the wonderful old doo-wop song *Blue Moon* was playing as performed by The Marcels.

When the music ended, he opened his eyes. On the ground, in addition to the body of poor Jerry, there lay sprawled, in grotesque poses, the two werewolves who were now back in their human form. Madame Astrelle was leaning against a rough wooden column, panting. Juan was leaning over her whispering. When she opened her eyes, he snapped at her neck and her warm blood flowed. Within seconds her head fell to the side. In spite of everything, she had been a beautiful woman.

Schnitzel looked at the scene, praying, unarmed. Tears streamed down his cheeks, and he smelled a little like shit. Poor fellow, he had survived after all.

Cliff did not give up his gun. He knew it was empty after having fired it repeatedly for all that time. The gun gave off a scorching heat and white smoke poured from the barrel.

Juan wiped the dust from his sleeves. The lights flickered. A stray bullet had hit a street lamp during the melee.

"Good work, gentlemen," he said.

"Get thee behind me!" stammered Cliff.

Juan laughed. "I'll stop. Try to get out of here as soon as possible. Around here they do not like a lot of firearms."

"But nobody came despite all the noise and mess we have made!"

"They are good-natured and drunkards, not stupid. Good night, gentlemen."

"Hey, you, stop!" said Cliff.

Juan, now on the threshold, turned back to look at Cliff. He lifted his chin defiantly.

"You're ... you're under gunpoint. You're not going anywhere!"

"When I was born, firearms had not yet been invented. Despite all the wounds caused by bullets, they heal just like wounds from any bladed weapon. Do you want to try again Clifford, you silly comic book peddler?"

Cliff moved his lips but said nothing. He dropped the gun and began to cry.

"Excuse us," said Schnitzel kneeling down beside Cliff.

Juan bowed. "Oh, and I recommend that the next time you buy a car, that you do not buy a yellow car, please."

I HATE TO GO
(New Edition)

CHAPTER ONE

I check one last time to make sure I've put everything in the bag. I hang it by the front door, to avoid coming down, getting in the taxi, and then realizing that I had forgotten my luggage. Then I go in the studio. I unzip the guitar case and pick up the mu guitar and check the tuning. Perfect. I walk back into the bedroom. Jamie is still sleeping, or pretending. I pinch the strings and begin to play.

"All my bags are packed, I'm ready to go..." I sing. I see a little smile appear on her face, still pretending to be asleep. I know I won't be able to finish the song before she opens her eyes and says...

"Are you really going to bring me the ring, this time?"

I put my guitar down and sit down beside her on the bed. "Hey, it's just a song!"

"All right, all right. This time where do you have to go?"

"I'm not sure I can tell you, you know that. We both know how angry your father gets if I violate his rules. I can only say that I won't be close to home."

Jamie stretches, then sits up in the bed, yawning. "My father, my father and my father. Just because I'm the boss's daughter, I sure would like to have some privilege to know where my man is going."

"Before I was your boyfriend, now I'm your man? Am I getting old?"

She ran a hand through my hair, messing it all up, and after it took me a lot of time to make it look just perfect, especially when I have to make a long journey. Oh well, I'll try to fix it again while I'm in the taxi.

"No, time seems to stand still," she says with a note of sadness and concern.

I look in the mirror, over her shoulder. In fact, we've been together for nearly five years, and I've changed very little. I winked, trying to reassure her. Jamie is also pretty much the same, with blond hair and crystal blue eyes. Her nose is still sprinkled with the small freckles that make her seem like a little girl. I wonder, at times, if it also affects my closeness to her.

The notorious beeeep of the taxi brings me back to reality. With nothing to do, I guess taxi drivers get a power play out of honking the damn horn until a passenger gets into the car. "I've got to go," I say.

"Okay," she says. "I beg you, please be careful Mr. Konopski."

"Be calm, Miss Hunter, I'll be home before I can call to say hello."

"Hello."

"Not that fast though."

I leave the house whistling a song, toting my suit bag slung over my left shoulder. I still wonder if what I put into it will be suitable for London's climate at this time of year.

"What's your opinion?" I ask the taxi driver. "Is it colder here or in London?"

The driver, an Indian with a turban on his head and a thick salt and pepper beard, shakes his head. "In London, you can count on it. My aunt, who lives there, always complains of the humidity and fog."

"Perfect. I've brought something suitable. I think."

My new friend then launches into an endless story of how he chose New York rather than Europe, about the things his aunt in London says, and a thousand other things. I'm always going to ask questions in these situations, try me.

A few hours later and I'm on the plane, heading toward Europe. I watch a movie, have something to munch on, and then bury myself in reading a dossier of the Foundation. At first glance, it might seem a trivial murder, nothing more. A rich man is found dead in his mansion with his throat slit open from side to side. The house, specify contacts in London, is in perfect condition. No signs of struggle, no forced entry. This would lead to the usual conclusion that the victim knew the assassin or murderers. This was also determined by the inspector... an Inspector Barnes. Before I read on, I look over the inspector's service record.

"That sucks," I say out loud, without realizing it.

"Pardon?" asks the guy in the seat next to me.

"I was saying, that sucks, I hate having to deal with *perfectionists*."

"Are you talking to me?"

"No, never mind. I was speaking of a co-worker... I'll have to meet in London. I can deduce from his curriculum that he will be a big pain in the ass. Excuse my language."

To be dressed so impeccably this guy must be a professional at whatever he does. My theory is he's probably a financial advisor.

"Financial Advisor?" I ask.

"Yes ... yes. You can tell?"

"A bit. Exactly what...?"

And here we are falling back into the old routine. The guy starts talking to me about global economy, emerging markets, and future projections... for the entire trip. Farewell then to the interesting dossier I was reading, although honestly, Mr. Hunter would crucify me if he saw me reading it publicly, especially in a confined space such as a corridor of airplane.

Patience, maybe I'll learn something about finance, while this plane zips it way across the ocean.

CHAPTER TWO

I arrive at Heathrow in the evening. I greet my fellow traveler farewell, thanking him for the knowledge that he gave me. Now, for at least a decade, I will not want to hear another word about finance. Without any checked luggage to have to deal with and my route already planned out on my tablet, a taxi will get me to the place in half an hour. I'll call Barnes once I arrive. I wouldn't want him to have to go to any trouble sending me a car to the airport, making me wait here. I hate to stand still, especially after flying for all those hours. In addition, I've got to close the matter at hand, before I can go home. After all, I promised my old pal, Steve that I would be home for the game, and to him that meant any game. While he ate, drank, and slept sports, I guess I should explain that, for me, sports only marginally interest me.

I hail a taxi, only giving the address and I point out that I care, because Inspector Barnes will be waiting for me. I don't know if it will work, but I show the driver the pass sent to me by Scotland Yard. That should deter him from trying to extend the route to squeeze more money out of me. I confess, I learned these tricks or rather I inherited them from my stays in Italy, with my maternal grandparents. Over there, it seems almost a habit.

The phone vibrates. It's my pal, crazy Steve. "Hola, amigo," I say.

"Hey! How 'bout six this afternoon?" says the other side of the phone, and the ocean.

"I think not."

"Job?"

"Work," I confirm.

He snorts. "You are lucky. The Chief always entrusts you to something stimulating, while we're walking the streets."

"Yeah, you know... what luck. I was hoping to get me a little R & R with Jamie and yet he sends me away."

Steve chuckles, blatantly taking me for a ride. "Come on, for solidarity old buddy, I'll drop by your place. Maybe I can be the interim Ray Konopski while you're away." I chuckle at his little joke.

"If *Mr. Hunter...*" I say chanting the name. He is still the closest thing to a father I have, "...sent me only, I think it's probably a simple case, right?"

There is moment of waiting on the other side, perhaps interference in the line. "Well, maybe. Just try to get back by next Sunday, okay? The *76ers* against the *Knicks*, and lots of beer."

Now there are two things I am sure of: a basketball game. And Steve. For nearly five years, he has been trying to convert me and make me cheer for the New York Knicks. Every so often, I give him satisfaction by pretending to follow the game with interest, but basically I'm only there for the company. And for the beer. But don't tell Steve or Jamie that, please.

"Old buddy, I'm going to cut you loose to avoid my usual huge phone bill."

"Hey, the Foundation pays you, right?"

"Well, yeah, but usually it's dinner with Mr. Hunter where I find myself more often than not," I point out.

"Haha... I get it! Anyway, let's get together for Sunday lunch. Only us little guys though. I'll call Luke."

"Sure thing. Bring whoever you want."

"You have no idea how much I envy you Ray. Have fun."

"Screw you, Steve."

"You're welcome."

CHAPTER THREE

The famous English fog. I never really understood what the difference was between this and the mist of the English countryside; the fact is that it is always a fascinating spectacle. Less gray than New York, the British capital has that charisma that comes from far away, and maybe I appreciate it even more given my European roots. I've seen similar landscapes in the periods I spent at my grandparents' house, in northern Italy. Wet autumns, where the sun disappeared in mid-afternoon, swallowed by a milky blanket. I'm a romantic, I know, at least that's what Jamie always says.

I get out of the taxi, waving to the good driver who left me in peace for the twenty-minute ride. I am grateful. I put the bag over my shoulder and head for the gate of the villa, enclosed by streams of yellow interim police tape. A couple of detectives stand guard at the entrance.

"Good evening," I begin by showing the pass. "Is Inspector Barnes inside?"

"No, I think he's at Central still. Should I call?" says one of them. A skinny little guy with reddish hair and a sharp nose like a pencil.

"It would be a good idea. Unless you want to come along and have a drink with me. I think that there is a well stocked bar inside."

The two look at me and then at each other. They seem embarrassed by my request, that or they had the same evil thoughts about having a drink. However, the redheaded one makes the call to the inspector. "In ten minutes he will be here, or so assured me."

"Can I ask you a favor?"

"What is it?"

"I have some homework to do, like reading a file. Could I go sit somewhere? Do you have a car I can use?"

Very gently, the redhead led me to the car and ushers me to sit inside. I can now retrieve a moment of lost time on the plane. Reviewing what I had already read, I'm snorting again over the "commendable conduct" of my new associate, Inspector Barnes.

I still wonder why the Foundation was involved, in a case that is really nothing to shout about. If I didn't know the moral integrity and the code that sets it apart, I would think that some wealthy relative has paid a lot of money to find out who did this, using our means, knowing it is much faster than the normal channels.

I cast a look at the villa. A beautiful country house, no doubt about it. At a guess, it has three times the rooms of the residence where Jamie and I live, and as many bathrooms as the Foundation's headquarters. I especially appreciate the style, exquisitely English, which always keeps that aspect inherited from the past, with towers and battlements, like a small castle or a fortified house. A large garden distances it from the main building walls, which are thick, at least a meter and a half.

Mr. Foster, Clark Foster, with his steel mills, has accumulated a nice nest egg over the last thirty years. No kids, two former wives, living with, definitely some *new tenant* of passage. Somehow, he tried to live in a safe. Yet, those thick walls do not seem to have served their purpose. That is the part that makes me suspicious. The retained security service, guaranteed by a renowned agency, had not been able to protect and prevent the murder. One of them was found in a daze, two more dead a few miles away.

Now I'm here. The curious detail, definitely omitted in the official statements, is the state in which the two agents were found.

"Good evening, Mr. Konopski," says a voice.

I look up and recognize Inspector Barnes. Hastily I put away the file and get out of the car, holding out my hand. In person the man is even more woodsy than I had evinced from the photos. He smells like talcum powder and barley candy.

"Good evening, Inspector. Sorry for the short notice."

"Don't worry, my boy," he says, inviting me to follow him to the house.

The redhead and his colleague separate, while Barnes opens the gate. Raising the police tape, we move on. Once inside, I can finally measure the grandeur of the house and its garden. The salary received by the Foundation would help me, I think, perhaps to buy only a fraction of such a house.

The driveway is not paved, but covered with fine white gravel that crunches underfoot. I notice the inspector is wearing impeccable English leather footwear. I make note there are some signs of wheel tracks, some automobile, others motorcycle.

"Mr. Foster was a motorcyclist?" I ask.

"Yes. We found a couple of Italian bikes in the garage."

"Ducati?"

"Exactly, yes."

A man of many words, this Barnes. Without asking more, we get inside the house. The interior, of course, is just as elegant as the exterior. Flipping the switch, Barnes turns on the lights. Only now I realize that one detective is following us. I look at him and he nods his head.

"Who's he?"

"Ah, detective Chapman."

"Hello detective Chapman. How are you doing?" I ask. I think he's more or less my age, give or take a few years, or from Jamie's satirical point-of-view, years younger.

"Good evening, sir," he says, snapping his heels. Sir... what's this guy take me for... his father?

"Look, there's no need to call me sir I..."

Barnes puts a hand on my arm. "Shall we continue, please?"

I would send him them both to hell, but then I would suffer the reproaches of Hunter so instead I just say, "Yeah, yeah, okay. Let's go."

Inspector *Sympathy* leads me to a door under the stairs. Anyone would have thought it was an easy entrance to a storage room, instead we are surprised to find behind the framework is a sophisticated push-button panel that, once a code is keyed in, reveals a secret passage with lots of stairs.

"Molto bello," I exclaim.

"Excuse me," asks Barnes.

"Yes, very nice. I mean, very nice."

When Barnes turns and goes, reassured by my more formal English reply, I wink at Chapman, who blurts out a smile.

We arrive in a living room, lit by several lamps on the walls, forged into the style of ancient torches. Various shrines, statues, armor, and other memorabilia fill the large room. Basically I see, a wet bar and a few couches, next to a beautiful pool table.

"The recreation room of Mr. Foster?" I ask.

"According to the testimony of the servants, but also by the previous wives of Mr. Foster, this was his personal guest room, of course restricted to the few who have had the good taste to appreciate the works it contains."

For Chapman, holding in his laughter almost deforms his mouth, it can't be easy keeping that oh so British stiff upper lip you know. For all the time that the inspector had been speaking, as he looked about the rooms, I have slightly teased him unawares, by mimicking his lip movement, giving me a serious look. I couldn't resist. I am lucky that he hasn't noticed.

"Have you surveyed the objects?" I ask.

"What, I'm sorry…?"

"You did take an inventory, just to see if something is missing, right?"

Barnes remains appalled. "N ... no. However, I can give you a short layout. I was already thinking the same thing, you know?"

"I don't doubt it. Let me know, okay?"

I take a few steps, always carrying the bag over my shoulder. I find the trace of chalk to indicate where the shape of Foster had been when he was found. Before him, there's a marble pedestal, which mimics an Ionic capital, and for some reason it is strangely empty.

"Was there something on top of this pedestal?" I ask Barnes.

"How so?" The inspector seems, to me, more and more disoriented.

"You will notice that there are other pedestals around the room, in addition to the display cases. Each of them has something on it."

Barnes looks around, through the eyes of one who sees the room for the first time. "Well, yes but the order seemed so random and heterogeneous that..."

"Don't worry. You have examined the security camera tape though?"

"Mr. Konopski, if we would have had the video that night, I think we should not have disturbed you, don't you agree?"

Desperate, I smack my forehead. I can't help myself. "Inspector, I did not mean it exactly that way, I wanted to know if you have seen the video before so that you can tell me what the hell was on the column!" I say this in such a manner, trying not to pass Barnes off for the idiot in the matter. Chapman would not want to lose this job...

CHAPTER FOUR

The hard drive on the top floor is intact. Whoever made the mess worked with the security cameras off for that evening. We see that the surveillance system is still in operation. I fumble a bit with the video. Barnes is standing right over me as I work. His hot breath is on my neck, and I feel a sort of anxiety, as if he is waiting for me to make a mistake so he can shout, "Ah-ha!" But I don't care and go on with my investigation.

"There it is!" I exclaim, pointing at the monitor. "A beautiful statue."

"And what would it be of?" asks Barnes approaching the screen.

I squeeze my eyes, sharpening the view. "Hard to say. Too far away, the image is grainy and not well enough defined for me to know."

"Hmm..." says Barnes.

"All we have to do is just check out the old records, to understand when it might have come into the house. Do we have a database?"

Barnes turns to Chapman, coughs and bounces on the balls of his feet a bit. The young officer shrugs, with huge embarrassment for his inspector.

Who the hell did they send me to deal with on this case, I wonder. On paper, Barnes is impeccable, perhaps because he's so far just been lucky or been given less complicated cases. Let's be honest, this does not seem to be that intricate. Yet, the inspector is lost in a glass of water.

"Okay, okay," he mumbles.

"Seek the point where it appears for the first time if you can, and let me know. Chapman, would you take care of this thing, please?"

"Just a moment. Let's put the record straight," Barnes intervenes. "This is my case, and these are my men. I should be the one to give the orders around here, if you please."

I shrug and curl my mouth, nodding my head as well. I know, I am disrespectful at times. "You are so right, I'm sorry. Would you then be so kind as to repeat to Chapman what I just asked of him?"

That said, I get up and leave the room, whistling a tune. It seems time to monitor the column more closely. If I were to elaborate only on the investigation and the work of these guys, I would not be going home before ten years. After all, they sent me here because I don't use their conventional methods, right?

Barnes feels embarrassed repeating my instructions to Chapman. After which he exits, climbing the stairs and calling, "Mr. Konopski, wait for me."

"Follow me Inspector, I'd like to finish a couple of things and then we can go get something to eat. I've made a trip of nearly eight hours, and I could not sleep on the plane, and right about now I'm starving."

Barnes puts a hand on my shoulder, stopping me. "Look, I understand that you have been called in by someone higher up, but you are not going to step over me on this."

He snorts, worse than a child. With a child it's okay to behave as a child, I think. But a man... I look him straight in the eye, hoping that he understands what I think. Seeing that empathy is in short supply with Barnes, I say: "Inspector, if you want to present your grievances, do it tomorrow, when I am less tired and more patient. I do not know how it is in these parts, but I'm used to playing with or without a team. In both cases, the job is always the same: I get to close a file, possibly do justice, and to prevent some debauched maniac from going around ripping people apart whenever they choose. So, and I am asking you as a personal favor, why don't you and I smoke the peace pipe, collaborate, and right now get out of here and go to dinner."

Barnes remains stunned. He says nothing. All he does is look at his watch, a brand new polished and flawless Graham chronograph. I'd like one as well, with the shiny stainless steel case, a truly modern classic. I will remember later to congratulate him on his choice of such a fine timepiece.

Back in the hall of the murder, I want to do an experiment, hoping that this will speed up the investigation. I open my bag, put on some headphones, and approach the pedestal. I connect headphones and press play on my cell phone.

"What are you doing?" asks Barnes, blinking.

"I'm listening to a little music."

"Now?"

"Yeah, it helps me work better."

I see him looking at me shocked. The white headphones with the black star must have upset him greatly. "Something wrong?" I ask.

"Well, your headphones…"

"Look, I know it may seem like an excuse, but these are my girlfriend's. Before I left, I tried to find my earplugs throughout the house. Are you married?"

Barnes frowns. "Yes, but what does that have to do with anything?"

"Great. So you know that when two people live together, things tend to take on a life of their own at home, moving mysteriously and suddenly disappearing. Well, I couldn't find my little black earplugs and I didn't have time to go out to buy a new pair. I settled for borrowing these from Jamie, who, by the way, will probably be pissed when she goes looking for them. I must remember to warn her. You know, this morning I forgot when I told her goodbye."

The good inspector just nods, looking more and more appalled. I'm playing an old song by *The Zombies* on my phone and enjoying the music. It helps me to concentrate. I know, when I'm away from Jamie, I tend to become melancholy and maudlin.

I put a hand on the stand and close my eyes. The presence of Barnes is too intrusive. "Do you mind?" I ask, gesturing him to move away a bit. The man did not even protest. Perhaps he has finally surrendered.

"Well let me tell you 'bout the way she looked, the way she'd act and the color of her hair, Her voice was soft and cool, Her eyes were clear and bright, but she's not there..." the singing brought me a sense of serenity, while the first images come into my mind.

CHAPTER FIVE

Well, I expected everything except finding a direct message from an old friend. The effrontery of those who committed this murder is out of the ordinary. Sure that he would come here, have given this sort of rendezvous, not caring that someone else, like myself, would use their skills to investigate, receiving the message. It is embarrassing, though it seems to have opened the mail for another person as well.

"Well?" Barnes asks.

"Yes?"

"What, what… tell me?"

"What do you want to know?"

"I do not know!" he says, raising his hands in despair. "You put on those silly headphones, listening to music and can determine..." he reaches out to touch a column, "…that a few nights ago, there may have sat a figurine on this bloody column that is now gone. And perhaps because of that, the assassin killed Mr. Foster."

I look at Barnes with approval. "Well done Inspector, precise and professional uniting clues, motive and everything that revolves around the case. Now, can I ask a favor?"

The Inspector stares and says in protest, "But I was questioning..."

"This isn't formal, come on. Must I have to ask how you are organized here; I have a question, quite urgent. I need to track down a car."

Barnes takes a handkerchief from his pocket, leans on a glass case, and wipes his forehead that has become beaded with sweat. I think if I wasn't with the Foundation, he would already have had a squad of little men in white shirts take me away for a straightjacket fitting.

"What car?" he asks, resigned.

"Do you want to write this down?"

Barnes nods and takes a notebook from inside his jacket pocket. Here is the professionalism of the Inspector, who now says,

"Okay, tell me."

"I need to know if, within a few miles, is housed a man with an old French car. A black Citroen DS, to be precise. Logically, to think, one that drives on the left, just to be accurate."

"And, the model Citroën is… BS?"

"No, no, listen okay? DS. Denver, Seattle."

"What is the license plate?"

"Oh my, not that. I think it is a European license plate, German maybe."

Barnes writes everything down methodically. He seems almost relaxed now. I know he I'm taking crazy. He'll never believe the truth when revealed. I would like to examine his mind, but I probably wouldn't like what I would see. And, after all, it would be unethical and unprofessional.

"I need to know something else too."

"I'm all ears," says Barnes.

"Are there many auction houses in London?"

"There are, God forbid. The most famous is…"

"No, no, excuse me for interrupting. Not auction houses, let's say, something more underground. A bit less official, where I could find stolen relics."

Scratching his head, the inspector looks for something in his pocket. "Do you mind if I go out to smoke for a moment?"

"Just think… I'll come too. Can I have one?"

We go outdoors. Despite my intense hunger, I want to smoke a cigarette. Since I arrived, I've forgotten my vice, one of many, just so you know. Barnes hands me a cigarette, *Benson & Hedges*, a good English smoke.

"You know, Mr. Foster was well received in London. A British Conservative, an excellent businessman, a benefactor who left millions of pounds into the coffers of the state, and he happily gave to charities. Now, if there were even the slightest suspicion that he was dealing with the trafficking of stolen items, it would be a big problem."

I take a deep breath, and say logically what comes immediately and say logically what come immediately into my head. My stomach is grumbling, and my insides beg me to give some leeway to Barnes. But I don't always listen to my gut. "Inspector, the statue was stolen, and that's probably why Foster was murdered, because he had an object that cannot be held legally. If we think, the museum room was not there in plain sight for anyone to go and find our tycoon, what do you say?"

"Well, maybe for security reasons…"

"Yeah, yeah, sure. Do me the courtesy to investigate along this track, okay?"

"Yes, I shall. In the meantime, what will you be doing?"

"When you've found the car, I will contact its owner. The assassin left a message for him." That said, I tossed my cigarette butt, stubbed it out, left him, and returned to pick up my bag.

Chapman gives me a ride to the hotel room. I get to take a relaxing hot shower, then change and go out again. A brisk walk and grabbing a bite to eat on the fly, in the hope of having a stroke of luck, will help me to feel less fatigued. I know I should not use my skills when I'm tired, but I am in a hurry to close the matter.

I stop at a restaurant in Covent Garden, the same place where I ate with Jamie a couple of years ago. I sit and imagine that she is here with me now, like that day. I try to remember that night, which we enjoyed, for the first time, our first trip outside the U.S. together. I've always promised myself to take her to Italy, to visit my mother's home, but you know, time passes until one day you wake up and realize you don't have enough time to do everything you hope to do.

"Your choice?" asks the waitress.

"Fish and chips. And a beer, of your choice."

A shot of calories is what I need. I look out the window, watching the night sky over Covent Garden become increasingly gray. The fog hides everything now, leaving me to just make out a few lights from the passing cars. Hell, even I had a stroke of luck in breeding.

At the moment my mind is not on the case. I'm starved and will confine myself to eating the food the waitress has just sat before me. And, of course, drinking this dense, dark beer with a name on the label I've never heard of before.

CHAPTER SIX

The phone rings. Jumping up in bed, I look around quickly and grab the cell phone off the nightstand. It takes me a moment to focus on the situation, and remember where I am and why. The display shows a number I don't know. I reply.

"Yes?"

"Mr. Konopski?" asks a voice from the other end.

"It's me."

"Ah, good. This is detective Chapman. I have just been notified that the car you are looking for has been spotted."

Yawn. "Very well, detective Chapman, and where is it?"

"One of the other detectives, Evans, saw it arrive while he was guarding the house. It stopped across the street, and then it immediately drove away."

Out of curiosity, before making any decision, I look at the clock. It is two in the morning, not an ideal time to take a scamper through the streets of London. Yawning again, and rubbing my eyes I ask, "Have you been following?"

"Of course!" says the detective proudly. "It went to a hotel in Covent Garden, in the neighborhood…"

"Yes, yes, I know where, Chapman." That bit of information suggested that I was on the right track. Fortunately or not, I just missed the appointment.

"Should we have them brought in?"

"No, no, that's not necessary. I will go personally to deal with it tomorrow night."

Chapman from the other end mumbles something. I sense his astonishment. "But really… you want to wait until tomorrow night?"

"Sure. At best, let me ask a favor, keep me updated on his possible movements. I will be at the hotel around six thirty tomorrow afternoon. Okay?"

"Well… okay then. Will do."

I leave Chapman disappointed and go back to sleep happy, almost. Falling back to sleep is not easy at first. I hook Jamie's headphones up to my phone and listen to a little music. Gradually, I slide back to sleep, while I plan the next day's activities. It would be a good idea that I meet my friend before sunset. Otherwise there could be trouble. I'm going to need to find him at exactly the time given to Chapman. I'm also sure that, despite the precautions and professionalism, he will have noticed the detectives who followed him. Knowing him, he won't give them any importance. Indeed, he will continue his business by ignoring them completely. Provided that they do not annoy him. But I have to ask myself... have they annoyed him yet?

The diligent Chapman calls me at exactly six o'clock, to confirm that our friend has not left yet, and the car is still parked outside the hotel. In turn, Inspector Barnes has not contacted me as of yet. I don't care, instead trusting in the support of detective Chapman, a man definitely willing to do the duty of good soldier, take a medal, and fulfill the task entrusted to him by his superior, an idiotic inspector, who is probably offended by my presence on the case. Poor Barnes, I could talk to him and tell him honestly who and what's in the middle of this thing but he would never believe me. I would pray that he could be left completely out of the case, and that he would retire in a country village somewhere far away from me.

"Chapman, should I take a taxi, or do you have someone who can pick me up?"

"I can send Evans, if he wants to."

"Chapman, can I ask you a question?"

"Yes, of coarse. What is it?"

"Are you and Evans the only detectives on this case other than the inspector?"

"No, but Evans is already in Covent Garden with Mitchell. He's nearby."

"The important thing is that someone stays there."

"Don't worry, Evans will at your hotel in under ten minutes."

Evans is one of those special detectives who are in the service for a lifetime but who manages to stay stuck to one level, just higher than a traffic cop. He's a prime example of submissiveness and fatalism being a common man, so much so that it's a wonder why he hasn't chosen a different job. In short, he doesn't get my jokes, doesn't smoke, moves slowly, and he drives with unexceptionable caution. He also doesn't use the siren even when really should. Oh, about my jokes, I find it kind of strange that Evans doesn't understand them. I am, after all, very funny, thank you.

"Good evening Mitchell. It is Mitchell, right?" I ask the detective who's on duty guarding the place when we arrive. Tall, lanky with protruding ears, Mitchell is as stiff as the seat of the car I just got out of. At least he's young and can hopefully aspire to something better than Evans.

"Yes, M'lord," he says, giving me a funny military salute.

"Our man?"

"He's still in there, but the light has gone out of his room."

I'm surprised. They even dared to find out which room he is in. If I had candy, I would give these two bold detectives a piece.

"Well, good job. Wait here," I say heading to the entrance.

"Don't you want us to come with you?"

I shake my head. "No, no, go figure. The man in there is neither dangerous nor is he involved with the murder."

"Are you sure?"

"Yes, I am," I reply. I hope I'm not wrong.

CHAPTER SEVEN

I enter the lobby. The hotel is like my friend, a good balance between luxury and sobriety. The decor is classic, inherited from the old and beautiful Victorian London, at least in style. Maybe even some of the furniture is original. I just need to do a search to find him and find him quickly. I half expect to see men in frock coats and top hats, wandering through the rooms. Instead a man in a black suit and striped tie, who you might call regimental, greets me. He looks at me from head to toe, his nostrils dilated in irritation.

"What can I do for... *you*?" he asks, seemingly annoyed by my presence.

Okay, I admit that I should have taken care of my appearance for this afternoon, wearing something different from the usual jeans and jacket from the university, but heck, it's my style and I'm comfortable. "Yes, please forgive me. I'm looking for a friend."

The guy responds with something that sounds like an "umpf" or a "tze". Then, remembering his professionalism, he decides to give me an answer. "Are you sure that this person is staying... *here*?"

"Yes, yes. I made an appointment. You know, we're going to talk business."

"What is the party's name?"

Here is the best part. What will he be called now? What name will he use? Not being sure I say, "Well, he's around six and a half feet tall, with long, black wavy hair. He sometimes talks to himself..."

"You mean you do not know the name of your friend?"

"Well... well..." Annoyed, I pull out a card. "Look, I'm here on behalf of Scotland Yard, so don't waste any more of my time. Tell me the room and get over it."

The man, seeing the card, immediately changes his expression and attitude. "Yes sir, excuse me. But really, I do not know how to help you without a name. We have a lot of people staying here, understand me when I say that it's hard to remember them all?"

After all, he's not wrong. "In short, the room number is seventy-seven."

"But that's the same man who the detectives asked about last night. They tracked him down with the car description. Every car has an identification number that corresponds to the room," he said smugly.

The car. I had forgotten about it. "Well, tell this man I'll be waiting for him here at the bar. I want you to taka note to him. And will you please do me the courtesy of letting me know when he comes down?"

"Yes sir."

"Can I get a drink now?"

"Yes sir. Please come in."

I scribble a message to my friend, and then I go to the bar to grab a drink and kill time. I'm sure that he'll come down soon and that he will want to talk with me.

I wait ten minutes, and he comes just as expected into the hotel bar. I get up when he comes toward me. It is most remarkable. He always seems the same, dressed in the usual way. I give him a nod that is not reciprocated.

"Konopski," he says with that low baritone voice. I can't tell if it's a greeting or a curse.

"Juan! How nice to see you again. Can I order you something to drink?"

"What do you want with me," he says. So far... so good. He sits down laying his bag on the ground, between his legs. He has eyes of darkness, one might say. Despite the light, I can't see his pupils.

"I'm glad you decided to meet me."

"Did I have a choice?"

"Well, you could go to the house, enter in, get alone with the message and go on to recover whatever interested you. That is one thing that you know that I still don't."

The waiter arrives, places a glass before Juan and slips away. The aura of Juan, especially when he does not want people around, becomes heavy. It is palpable and I can perceive it myself. I admit that I would much rather be somewhere else right now.

"I avoid unnecessary effort, right? Or so you said."

"Well, let's get down to business. Jamaine... Jamaine, do you know him?"

Juan grins. "Ah, then Jamaine has come out into the open then."

"Then you know him. Well, he left a message for me regarding the theft of the item from the villa. You know what that is, right?"

Juan looks around, takes a sip from his glass and crosses his legs. "It's needless to hide something, right Ray?"

"Right." Juan knows me, knows that I have seen it all, and knows what I can do. I am nothing compared to his skills, but I know enough that it allowed me to see the message left by this Jamaine.

"A statue, that you may have seen, is a... let's call it a demon. To be precise, it is *Baphomet*. It dates from the late 17th century, so it is ancient. It has a special feature, however: It contains an ingenious treasure chest, the key of which is represented by the horns."

Making a mental note, I don't remember seeing the horns. In truth, I saw very little of the object, because that devil, Jamaine kept it well covered, and even in the video footage you would have to guess that particular. "Horns?"

"Yes, the horns when embedded into the head of the goat make a delicate mechanism turn allowing the head to be removed."

I finish my glass, throwing a look towards the entrance of the bar. A woman was about to enter, but she shook her head as if something had annoyed her. Then she retraced her steps, leaving the bar. On other occasions, the result would have been different, but obviously, at this time, Juan was more interested in the statue than any woman.

"And where are the horns?"

"I bought them myself, weeks ago at an auction, here in England. This old nation has more than one object that interests me."

As he says that he joins his hands together clasping his fingers. I keep my eyes on his hands. They might do unexpected things. Some time ago, he said something that made me respect him by reassuring me that he would not harm me. From there he went on to consider our relationship a friendship, but it is impossible for me to relax with a character like him in my presence.

"Why did not you buy the statue, then?"

"Something went wrong. The auction started an hour early. It does not take much imagination to suppose that Jamaine anticipated the time on purpose, so that he was certain that someone else bought it."

"Sorry, I'm missing something though. Jamaine couldn't buy it directly?"

"Surely you can determine the reason?"

In all honesty, I don't know this Jamaine, although I gather from some of the details I've read what sort of creature he is. I wanted to risk knowing more than what was on paper, hoping to find out from Juan the information that I had missed. Making it clear that I don't know some things would put me at a disadvantage. But I yield anyway. "No, I admit that I don't."

Juan gives a nod to the waiter, who seems intuitive to what he wants. He rushes to our table with a full bottle of *Disaronno*, unopened, leaving it on the table and walks away.

"You have excellent taste, I see," I say.

"I feel like something sweet."

I pour half a glass. I drink while I wait for him to finally explain some things to me.

"Let me be brief, Konopski. Jamaine is a member of a French family of werewolves, and he is also one of their idiots. The generations have coupled through inbreeding and it must have brought some deficiency within their genetic code. I stand corrected. Now that I think of it, he is the second most idiotic member, after his sister, Astrelle, who tried to catch me in a trap recently."

I swallow the liquor and nod. "I heard something about it. That was you?"

"I acted in self-defense."

"I don't doubt it. So you say you Jamaine did…"

"He acted out of revenge because he is an imbecile. His modus operandi could have landed him in really big trouble. Not all of us are as patient as me."

Said by him, the phrase sounds strange. He would never give the impression of a meek person, one who sits in a corner quietly so as not to be observed. Often, over the years, I have heard things really disturbing and macabre concerning Juan. The stories and dossier on him have made me shudder at times, at least until I met him. From then on it has become even worse.

"Well, do you mean to accept the invitation?"

"Why shouldn't I?"

"I know you will too, although I should give you a lecture on prudence, balance and other things like that."

Juan smiles. I have to wonder if he's listening to the voice of the Elder. So I ask, "Is the Old Man here?"

"Yes, and he greets you. He is very paternalistic, in fact, he is pleased that we are already thinking of him."

The story of Juan and the Elder, as he calls him, began so long ago, that the story turns up in the very first dossier. More than once, some careful observer could see Juan absorbed, as if listening to someone and answering. I am one of the few who knows the truth about his companion... this spirit, if it can be defined as such. "I think you mean Jamaine would get you in trouble with normal society, and that it would also involve the police. This could be the reason, right?"

"Two or three policemen are not going to change my life. I suppose, however, now that you're involved, you should, at least, close the case. This would mean, if I know you, that I can follow your own request in order to somehow deliver the guilty party. Am I correct?"

This time I smile, gambling a bit. "Almost correct. Mine is *not* a request, Juan. So I'll just come with you."

CHAPTER EIGHT

I walk away and light up a cigarette. I see Mitchell, on the other side of the road, with his idiot partner in the seat next to him, the car and both men lit by a yellowish streetlight. Of course they don't know how to get noticed, those two. I chuckle as I walk over to join them, finishing the cigarette before getting into the car. Slightly tipsy, after all those glasses of liquor, I know that by chatting I can exhaust these two bold agents.

"Good evening," begins Mitchell.

"Hi guys. Everything's okay. You can take me back to my hotel."

Mitchell reacts as expected. Evans looks at me questioningly. He shrugs and goes back to concentrating on the phone. Maybe he did something wrong, and he's apologizing to his wife. "Have I been keeping you waiting too long?" I ask.

"It's no bother. Did you speak to our man? "Mitchell gets right to the point.

"Yeah, yeah, all right. I delivered the message, I told him to remain available and all that other applicable *bla bla*. He said that he would be happy to cooperate if we need him."

I lean toward Evans intrigued. "What's up with your partner here? He in trouble?"

Embarrassed, Evans tries to hide the phone. "Um..."

"I like it, can I pass that saying on? Sometimes I really need to empty my brain you know, and using that word seems like a great way to do it."

Without another word, Mitchell starts the car and takes me back to the hotel. On the way, of course, I give them the honor of listening to me talk and telling them about the two things that I certainly don't need. I've done well, and that's exactly what I wanted to do. If I don't want any reciprocal conversation I just speak in bursts to prevent the other person from intervening. Especially when I don't intend to follow their directives on the case.

Juan said he would pick me up after midnight. I trust him. He's an honorable man who keeps his word. I relax looking at the TV, while eating something that I picked up and brought to my room. Usually I avoid eating before a mission, but I have to absorb the alcohol that I took in earlier. Juan can drink like a sponge, without suffering any aftereffects. I wonder, after all, what *can* harm him or have any kind of ill effect on him.

I go out on the balcony to smoke a cigarette, watching every car that passes below, hoping to see her arrive. In heaven, as designed by this Jamaine character, a full moon, stars, and this crap about werewolves all play a part. It's really theatrical. Jamaine, really, I've got nothing to say, as if we really need a bright ball in the sky to cause us to mutate and become *really bad.*

The phone vibrates. It's Juan. I look out the window and see him on the sidewalk, walking in front of the restaurant opposite. We look at each other and nod, and then I go down to meet him.

"Here I am," I say to Juan. "Do you want to walk?"

He beckons me to follow him into a nearby alley. The Citroën is there waiting for us, hidden in the dark. I can see the moon's reflection on its sleek body.

"You have weapons," he asks once we are in the car.

"No, I don't. I could have asked for a gun from Inspector Barnes, but you agree with me that it would be useless, right?"

He nods. "There are always the servants. Not all of them are mongrels."

"I think I can handle the humans. You have something?"

"Nothing in particular."

"I'd be curious to see what this *nothing in particular* is."

Juan brings the car out into traffic, heading for the suburbs. "I think, basically, we use, more or less, the same means, right?"

Of course, the difference is that Juan has far more experience than me. Who knows how long he's been at it. I absorbed these abilities by chance, or by misfortune, according to some people.

"I'm not at your level, but I'm getting better. You'll see."

"That is good to hear. The last time I saw you in action," he says, "you had some gaps to fill. I hope you will be well exercised."

"It's no longer the time of the great sorcerers, is it?"

"The Masters are almost extinct," he says, with that voice from beyond the grave.

"How many are there? Do you have an estimate?"

Juan protrudes his lower lip, and nods his head. "I'd say about six or seven at the most. There used to be around two hundred in the olden days."

"You have taken *Lantaurion* away from your calculation, haven't you?"

"Yes."

I still can't fathom the fact of being able to confront and eliminate Lantaurion, one of the Witchcraft Masters with his thousand-man army. But that's another story, besides we're still in the middle of this one.

"And the other one hundred and ninety-nine, how about them?" I ask.

"I killed them myself," he says.

I hate it when he's so cocky. "Surely you're exaggerating!"

"You think?" he says, and as he says it I zero in on those two dark caves where his eyes are hidden. I decide I don't want to question him further.

CHAPTER NINE

Juan seems relaxed. He's in no hurry. It makes sense for someone who has something like eternity before him. You might think that he's taking his time to devise a plan, but I bet he already has the whole picture of the situation before his eyes. That makes me feel safe, like a child with his father. I can be a bit arrogant and full of myself sometimes, and a bit too brazen, just like Mr. Hunter, Jamie's father, but this time I can afford to be. Juan has survived the most diabolical things, harmful, dangerous and ferocious, that Heaven, Earth and the Underworld has ever seen.

"What are you…?" I ask.

What am I what?"

"No, I'm sorry, I was thinking aloud. What are you thinking to do once we get there? What I mean is, are you thinking about doing some of your slaughter and carnage stuff, and then taking the statue with us?"

Juan whistles. "I was thinking of something more elegant, but your suggestion will be taken into account. As to your query about the statue, well, that I need that for my own purposes."

This is a fine mess. To close the matter and make Barnes happy with his standing in the Yard, I should, at least, bring back the statue and some evidence that this Jamaine character, killed our moneybags. "Do you need the whole statue?"

"Tell you what, Ray. I take what is inside and you can have the statue. Okay?"

While he tells me this, he stops at a traffic light and looks me in the eyes. The red light is reflected in his eyes, and for once I can see his pupils. Funny, it's still impossible for me to tell the color of his irises. Once again.

"I won't ask what's inside."

"Bravo."

In less than an hour, we're out of London, surrounded by the green areas of the English countryside. The fog makes us a partner, and Juan has become even more cautious in his driving. I don't think that the theme of dying or getting hurt bothers him at all, but rather if I remember correctly, it's that he has a kind of adoration for this car.

We stop after taking a left turn, far into the depths of this rural area. There are hints of houses and lights around us, except ahead I see there's a distinct yet dim luminescence a short way from where we've stopped.

"We'll go on foot from here," says Juan.

I open the door with caution. Immediately moisture grips me, making me shiver. I cover my head with the hood of my sweatshirt and follow my friend, already walking toward the small light. Finally the mystery is solved. We are faced with an old rusty gate, lit by a small Victorian lantern. A sign bears a name but that doesn't tell me anything.

"Are you sure we're at the right place?"

"You said that the message was waiting for me at the country estate. The family of Jamaine has only this place in London. Also, if you had followed the case and read the best dossier, you'd notice that the bodies of the two guards were found at the stream, but we've been through this before."

I nod. "Yes, you're right, of course."

My phone rings. Juan looks at me and shakes his head. The display shows a number that I don't know. "Hello?" I say.

"Konopski! Where the hell are you?" said a voice on the other side.

"Whom am I speaking with?"

"I am Inspector Barnes. I've been expecting a report, help, anything. Instead you enter the hotel, talk with a man that has been indicated as being involved in the case, and then you disappear!"

I pretend a yawn. "Inspector, Inspector. I found who I was looking for. Look, give me some time now, at least half a day, and I will have a detailed report on the matter. Right now, I'm a little tired. Do you mind?"

Barnes grumbles from the other end. Juan beckons me to cut the call short, and without waiting, presses the doorbell. A metallic sound warns us that we have opened the gate.

"Inspector, really, I have to go. It was a pleasure chatting with you."

"Konopski, I wanted to also say that we have no news of any auction, at least of those who would talk with us."

"It's nothing, nothing. Now if you don't want anything else of me. Good night."

I am finally free and I follow Juan, who is as calm as if he were at his own home, walking along the path to the house. In the fog, I can imagine the silhouette of a large building. The spires of the roof stand out on the squared perimeter. Some lights from large windows begin to appear. My friend pauses for a moment, fiddling with something that he has around his neck and then bends down as if to depose of an object on the ground. Without saying anything, he raises back up and continues walking, muttering words that I don't understand. But I know that it's better for me to remain silent at this time, and it is a suggestion that comes from inside, I don't know where, although I think it has to do with memories inherited from Lantaurion.

"Some kind of insurance," he says, breaking the silence with a succinct explanation.

"I see."

"Sometimes I like to have my back covered."

"Okay," I say as I turn around to look behind us. It's very dark and I can't see anything.

We arrive at the portico, where there are two thugs waiting with crossed arms. They nod for us to follow them, and we follow. Inside, the warmth of the room warms me and seems to shake off moisture that I accumulated. A fireplace in a sidewall of the wide hall is the source of this pleasant heat, so great that we could probably cook a whole pig.

At the stairs, stand a row of men. A man is descending the stairs and he's applauded as he arrives on the ground floor. He sports a trimmed beard, thick and curly hair, with bushy eyebrows pressed together, not trying to hide his true nature. The others who follow him seem like reproductions of the same man.

"Ricardo Juan Ramon de la Pasión. A real honor to have you here with us," the man says. He shakes hands with Juan, like one of those toy monkeys with the clapping saucers. I find it Irritating.

"Jamaine, the honor is all mine," replied my friend.

"But you... do you really have all those names?" I ask Juan. Jamaine notices me and gives me an interrogative look, and then he sends the same look to Juan. "And the wren here, who would he be?"

"Ah, excuse the rudeness. I brought an old friend. I hope you do not mind."

The man looks at his companions, who are now taking up strategic positions in the room, around the perimeter. "No, not really. Can I offer you something, before we talk business?"

"Do you want something, Ray?" Juan asks.

"If Mr. Jamaine doesn't mind, I'll have a glass of brandy. Or better yet, if the cognac is excellent, since it originates from ... yes, Mr. ... er ... Jamaine's home country."

Jamaine looks at me searchingly. He holds out his hand. "I have the pleasure of speaking with Mr.—?"

"Ray Konopski," I reply, accepting his hand.

"Konopski, Konopski, Konopski. Let me think. The name is familiar to me. Are you familiar with the name, Albéric?" he says pointing to the guy closest to him.

Albéric thinks for a bit. "Yes, he should be the American who was dealing with that witch doctor a couple of years ago."

"Can you be more specific?"

"Some wizard who moved to New York and decided to cooperate with the underworld there. Landurion, I think he was called."

"Listen guys, I can understand your language and maybe I can screw up a pronunciation but the name is Lantaurion to be accurate."

"Yes, he's correct," says Albéric. I will remember that man's arrogance later.

"Well," says Jamaine. "It's a pleasure to have you here. I hope you will consider me a gracious host like Juan," he says with a smile, watching his cronies. Without another word, he whistles. From a door, next to the fireplace, a comely girl comes out dressed very theatrically in a sheer nighty with lace and white trim. She's pushing a liquor cart full of bottles and clinking glasses. Yes,

Jamaine is just as described by Juan, a braggart who believes he lives in an old movie.

The girl doesn't appear to be frightened, she asks me something, I think she speaking French. I look at Juan, but he ignores me.

"Cognac?" I reply. I think she must have guessed, because the girl takes a bottle of Remy Martin and pours me half a glass. "Merci," I say. One of the few words I truly know in French. My little show from a moment ago was just that... a show.

Juan declines, instead he talks to Jamaine. I am the only one drinking. "Let us get to the point, Jamaine. What is the reason for your call?"

"You did see the message, no?"

"No, he didn't. I reported it to him," I said.

The smile on the face of the werewolf, Jamaine, now looks very grim. Not that he scares me, God forbid. Rather, it makes me a little ballsy for my presumption, but after all, we are in his house. "I got the message before him," I say with a shrug.

"This is unseemly. It's like listening to someone else's voicemail. Is this man your butler, Juan?"

"No, and I trust him."

Jamaine views the bag Juan has with him. "You brought the horns?"

"No."

"I told you to bring them."

I almost drown myself with Cognac. "Oh shit. Excuse me Juan. I forgot to tell you to bring the horns. The fact is that when I got the message, I didn't know about the horns and the rest. Excuse me, okay?"

Jamaine's chest swells so much that I believe he'll explode at least a couple of shirt buttons. He doesn't seem to like the news, nor does he accept my apologies, he advances towards me, a little threatening, blowing like a bull.

Juan stops him, by placing a hand on his chest. "Hey, put on the brakes. I would not bring it anyway. I'm not that stupid."

"Really? But I think you are. I ... I had an agreement to propose with you and..."

"Jamaine, get it over with. Go ahead and send your friend away. The one watching from the top of the stairs. I suppose you know by now that we know what you want to do with the horns. You should thank me."

From the stairs, appears another guy, applauding him as well. What the hell! Why do they all applaud this freak? I look up at the man and frame him for a few moments: a middle-aged man, plump, greased up the spine. A big amulet, embarrassingly gaudy, hangs from his swollen chest. "Juan, why are we supposed to thank you?" he asks.

"Viduus, nice to see you," says Juan calmly. "I have saved you from what's inside the statue, you understand?"

There are moments when you can feel that something big is about to demolish the environment, an event that would change the apparent tranquility of this scene. Well, I feel that now, prior to any human knowledge. For safety, I generally seek music as a solace. I rejoice to see, on the wall behind me, a good stereo, and while everyone's focus is on the fat guy coming down the stairs, I walk over to the stereo. Hello and welcome to a party, I think.

"Do you mind if I put on this record…?" I ask.

Jamaine looks back at me, just as I put the CD in the drive.

CHAPTER TEN

The mega collection of The Zombies, *Zombie Heaven*, caught my attention immediately. If I weren't the gentleman that I am, I would have already slipped it into my bag. While the notes of *She's Not There* fill the room, I turn and see who's watching me. I don't know if I read curiosity on their faces or what, so much so that I feel compelled to say something.

"You don't mind do you?"

Jamaine, eyes bulging, seeks an explanation from Juan, who simply passes a hand over his eyes.

"Mr. Konopski, we are here discussing serious things. We're not playing!" exclaims Jamaine, with that professor-like tone I can't stand.

"Yeah, yeah, all right, but a little music can relax the nerves during the trading day, trust me, dear Jamaine."

Incredulous, the man turns back to Juan. "We'll talk about that as well. Afterward. Now back to the topic before we were interrupted. My sister, Madame Astrelle, was found south of London, in a village lost in the heather. Too bad she was dead, she and two other members of my family. Someone, who says he was looking for Viduus confirmed to me that you might have something to do with it. Who should I believe?"

Juan turned his head, to the right and to the left. Jamaine and Albéric seem to be on guard, ready to leap. Watching them carefully, I can see something in them mutating. They are getting hairy too and the sclera of their eyes has turned yellow, crossed by red veins. It looks like a bad sign.

"Jamaine, you know that your sister tried to lead me into a trap, right? This was not like her at all. But it fits you very well. You know, I am convinced that she acted according to your own design, but it seems, as often happens in these things, you're not well understood."

Viduus takes a step down the stairs, and clears his throat. "Juan, Juan, Juan. I think you're not in the position to raise the tone of your voice. Jamaine has been far too kind in welcoming you into his home and in seeking a compromise, has he not?"

"And the agreement would be what? For me to give you the ability to open the statue, pull out the sheet, and summon a demon? Jamaine, do you even know what the real intentions of Viduus are?"

Jamaine briefly betrays his ignorance. It is clear that he didn't know about this particular. "What...? Juan, I do not care what you have to say. Viduus has worked for my family for a long time. It is he who brings new followers and converts them. We were weakening, the bloodline becoming increasingly diluted. And it was he who brought new—"

"Jamaine. I do not care," interrupts Juan. "Let's finish this. Hand over the statue, let me open the door, and then forget about me."

There is a silence. Almost. *Tell her no*, with *no, no, no* repeated, seems to respond to Juan's request instead of Jamaine. And as I predicted, the climax is happening right now. The clothes are rent, and the howling covers the music. In a few moments, werewolves, in humanoid form, fangs and claws bared, will be ready to jump.

Juan doesn't waste time. While the two werewolves approach, a sound like crackling fire emits from his mouth. Immediately, the two are on fire, their fur suddenly aflame. Then, Juan whistles. The windows crash in and two dogs, as black as night and with eyes of ember, spring into the room.

I don't waste time either, searching in my mind for the right sound. I think of the wind, the cold winter wind blowing over the mountains and imitate it. I end up swirling, first landing on the stairs, in front of a surprised Viduus.

"You... you..." he stammers. "Your spell casting ability is worthless, your magic can not touch me."

"Spells no, but this can," I say, smashing an opened hand blow to his throat. It feels like his trachea was smashed. Viduus tries to say something but only red bubbles come forth from his lips. At least he won't be a bother voiceless. With the wizard out of action, I concentrate on helping Juan.

"Albéric!" I hear a scream. The voice must be my own. One of the wolves turns to me, and I understand that it is him. He takes four steps or so and I take my mind in his direction while he growls and shows his fangs.

I see Juan take out what I suppose is Jamaine, while two others are struggling with the dogs. The mysterious dark blades of my friend appear to have already opened several cuts on the monster that is bleeding profusely. Albéric, meanwhile, is almost on top of me. Repeating the first sound, I overcome him and suddenly appear behind him. In disbelief, he turns and finds me ready to fight back.

"What was that thing you did with the fire?" I call out to Juan. But he doesn't answer, and I have to figure my own way out of this. Sure of myself, I give it a try.

What comes out of my mouth is more like the flame from a gas stove than that of a disruptive forest fire. A sizzling sound and a smell of burnt hair stop Albéric for only a moment. His muzzle hair has just been scorched by a flame like that of a match. The werewolf's answer is to backhand me across the face, making me fall and slip for a few meters. Stunned I get up, just in time to see Albéric running on all fours towards me. His jaws are wide open suggesting that, in just a second my throat will be ripped out if I don't move fast. I use the same trick as before, and spin up, causing me to land on his back.

"Back to your doghouse, mutt!" I say slamming my two fists down on his head. I don't think he suffers much, but at least he looks surprised. Finally, I dig deep into my subconscious, and, maybe, I find what I need. While I struggle, supporting the palm of my left hand on his hairy skull, I think of winter ice, of something frozen. My voice becomes the crunch of a sheet of ice breaking, and Albéric slumps to the ground. The moment his head touches the ground, it shatters into a thousand pieces of tiny ice crystals.

Exhausted, I get up from the ground, almost slipping on of what remains of the head of the wolf. Juan is standing next to Viduus, a hand around his throat. Jamaine and the others are again in their human form, lying on the ground, stone dead. Juan's dogs are sniffing them. One of the dogs looks at me for a moment, and then goes to his master, followed by the other.

"Viduus, maybe you have something to tell me?" asks Juan,

squeezing the fat man's throat even tighter. He shakes his head, muttering a froth of red bubbles. Juan places two fingers to the guy's forehead, and his eyes are closed forever.

"Damn Juan, now we have to look all over for the statue. You know how big this house is? We better hope it's here!" I complain.

"I cannot say, my friend. I think I know of someone who can help though," he says, pointing to the girl, who is still standing at the door she had gone through before. I do not know exactly what she's thinking, but I'd say she's terrified."

"Oh, okay," I say. I get up and straighten my jacket and pants. I'm going to change CDs. The first one has finished.

CHAPTER ELEVEN

Juan put the horns in the statue, holding his breath. I hear the noise of a mechanism as it snaps in place, like a lock that opens, and the statue's head comes loose in Juan's hands. Inside, a roll of yellowed paper comes to light.

"Well, to me goes the piece of paper, and to you goes the statue. Do what you want with it," says Juan, pocketing the roll.

"I don't want to know what it is, just remount the head. I didn't see anything."

"Good boy. Now I believe that our roads should be divided. "

I'm relieved. My task is finished and I just have to call Barnes, make a report that will not be read by anyone who doesn't have the level required to access it, and everything will be resolved in an incidental murder case, following a quarrel between two businessmen over ownership of an ancient statue. The culprit will be the deceased Jamaine. Nothing difficult and the public will be satisfied, above all, to accuse a Frenchman of the crime. Strange people, these Brits.

"Where are you going now?"

"The Elder suggested I go to Italy. It seems that the boy is there now. He will be difficult to recognize. I'll be there for a few months, I think."

"Italy. I'd love to return. Perhaps I could bring Jamie, what do you say?"

Juan smiles at me, that way I don't yet know how to decipher. "Try not to get in my way *too* much, Konopski. Things are not always as simple as this evening."

"Ah, of course."

"I have to go now. You'll get back with your cop friends?"

"Yeah, they'll give me a ride. Until next time, Juan."

He climbs into the car. It starts up and he gives me a nod with his hand.

"Oh, Juan. One last thing!" I rush out to ask him before he's gone.

He lowers the window. "What is it now?"

"Where can I buy a decent ring here in London?"

Barnes arrives almost an hour later. Chapman is with him, along with forensic and other staff. I light up a cigarette while analyzing the scene and questioning the girl about how she ended up in this unique home. It turns out she was kidnapped in France, forcibly taken together with three other girls and brought here to England. Of the others, there's been no sign up until now.

Barnes comes to me. "Konopski, have you prepared a report?"

"Of course, you will have it tomorrow. You know I can't help but deliver it accurately, right?"

The inspector looks smaller now, knowing he was cut off from a big part of it. The populous won't know of course, the people will have to believe anything else; these are my directives regarding the matter. "Yes, yes. Let me have it… all. Do you need a ride?"

"Yes, I have to catch a plane to New York as soon as possible. Thank you."

What can I say? I'm the type guy that just likes being at home with my girl, Jamie. I hate to be apart from her.

TELL HIM

CHAPTER ONE

I wake up suddenly. The air enters into my lungs violently, a shot of oxygen that makes my eyes roll. *Not again...* I think. The touch of ashes where I am lying, naked, helps me to understand what has happened.

I stretch and relax my muscles and get off the table. The cellar is dark. From a small window, shuttered over with wooden planks, just a thread of light comes through. It's not nighttime, there is still some sunlight left. I just have to figure out which house I'm in, tidy up some, and get out.

I hear a lawnmower, a familiar sound that helps me determine where I am this time: *Harrow, Headstone Road.* That asshole Mr. Hutton is mowing his lawn, just as he does every other day.

I climb the stairs, unlock the security door and enter into the kitchen. What I need is to eat, take a shower and retrieve the car and my belongings. I open the fridge, and with joy I see that it's well stocked, at least as far as I'm concerned. Orange juice, eggs and bacon, just to start the day and give a little bit of energy to this tired body.

I give myself twenty minutes of time, including breakfast and a shower, and then I head to the bedroom. If I'm lucky, my cell phone is charged and can I call Central.

Bingo, it's charged. Using a hidden ID, I call the base. Officer Wool answers, with that smooth as silk *velvet voice*, as my colleagues like to call him I can't blame them. It's too bad that frequently hearing and seeing someone doesn't seem to match up and Officer Wool is certainly one of those cases.

"Wool? Yes, This is Jeff, Jeff Harper," I say.

"Hello Jeff. What can I do for you?" he replies with his best television voice.

"Can I talk to Maitland?"

"The deputy is out with Inspector Barnes."

"Shit!" I exclaim.

"What?"

"Nothing, it's nothing, I'm sorry. Do you know where I can find them?"

"Just a minute." I can tell he has laid the phone down and is clacking away on the keyboard. "He's at Lots Road."

My heart begins to beat faster. With all the places where they could be, why there I wonder?

"Lots Road? Why?"

Wool does not respond right away, he lets a few seconds pass which seems to me like years. "The old factory. There are bodies…"

"The one with the two chimneys?"

"I don't know. It just shows to me as an old factory. It just gives me the reference to coordinate the teams. "

"Thank you. You are very kind."

"But ... Jeff, you should be there too. Didn't you get the call?"

Of course I would have received it if I weren't such an idiot, it's too bad that my phone is in my damn car thirteen miles from where I am now. "Yeah, Wool. Unfortunately I'm having a problem with my phone again. I really need to get a new one. I mean, this morning I turned it on and off and I'm still waiting for the restart and face—"

"I understand," he interrupted. "But if I were you I would hurry up. They have a large team already mobilized."

"Why?"

"You'll find once you get there. It's time for me to leave you, sweetheart. Have a good day."

I was going to hang up, but I remembered something. "Oh, Wool..."

"Yeah…"

"Can I count on you to...?"

"Of course, as always. And as always you know what I want in return, right?"

A privileged birth has its advantages and its disadvantages.

CHAPTER TWO

Mylan, a damn good taxi driver and my trusted confidant, arrives on time. We nod agreement and he opens the rear door. "Good morning, Mr. Harper."

"Good morning to you, Mr. Mylan."

"Travel with ease this morning?"

"Not so much."

"I see. I will try to see you get to your destination in as much comfort as possible."

I would tell him to hurry up and not to break my balls, but I think it would spoil our friendship. You see we have an arrangement, he and I, for these occasions. He is silent about my quirks, and I close an eye on some of his bad habits. But there's really no need for this talking in code stuff... the old fart.

"Thanks, it's very kind of you."

He smiles at me from under his bushy, white eyebrows. He really should look reassuring with that bush of curly hair and the jacket and all, just as a good taxi driver should, and yet...

Thirty minutes exactly and we are outside the cafe where I left the car last night. I pay Mylan and recover my things from the vehicle.

"Holy shit!" I exclaim loudly, scaring two girls coming out of pub at that moment. Their eyes go wide. "Excuse me ladies. I just got a ticket. Funny, huh? I'm a cop and I get a traffic ticket!"

They hurry away, maybe even more frightened by my behavior. Ah, to hell with them! Now I have to figure out how to justify my car being here, because half Central will know about the ticket within a few hours.

I turn on the phone. The time activates the reception and with that comes all of my messages and missed calls. I give Chapman, the quietest guy around Barnes I can think of, a call.

"Hey, I got the message," I say.

"Where are you? Barnes has not really noticed yet but he will soon, as soon as he's done mapping out the murder scene, he'll give me instructions and I assure you he will be a bitter cock about missing the call. Tell me you're already here."

"I'm in front of Fairbanks. I left the car parked there. I'll go on foot."

"No, no, come by car, right away. The gates are open and you can drive in. Hurry up. It's a mess around here."

I'm in utter misery. I get in the car, enter into traffic and I'm soon at the factory. I don't need to figure it out; I can see my uniformed colleagues stationed at the entrance that's cordoned off with yellow police tape. There are also a couple of ambulances in the courtyard and, judging by the fact that the drivers are smoking, leaning against their vehicle, I can understand that anyone who was in the factory last night suffered a fate similar to mine, without my special advantages, though.

Chapman sees me and approaches. Barnes and Maitland are talking to the coroner and they don't notice me yet.

"There you are!" he says.

Perkins and Bellman give me a look and laugh quietly between themselves. "What the hell are those two morons laughing about?" I ask.

Chapman beckons me to leave it alone. "I'll summarize what's happened and what..."

"No, what the hell are they laughing at?"

"Well, I guess your excuse about the phone problems don't hold water by the fact that your car was ticketed earlier by Fairbanks. They told me that the ticket on your windshield carries a fine of nearly two hundred Sterling."

"Fuck you."

"I do not know what you did over there last night, but if by any chance you noticed something that might be helpful you ought to tell Maitland, before he asks you."

I throw a glance at Barnes and he noted my arrival. Maitland nods to me inviting me to join them. I run my fingers through my hair and ask Chapman, "You got a cigarette?"

"Yes but..."

"The hell with them. I don't think my cigarette will pollute the crime scene. Look how small this place is."

The factory is empty and anything but small. The only things remaining are the skeletons of old machinery, a rusted flight of stairs leading to the offices, a lot of dust on the red stone floor, and a mattress brought in by guests who sleep here at night. Poor devils.

"Good morning," I say approaching.

"Harper, are you sure you were finished?" asks Maitland. You look like you were yanked out of bed by force. Maitland's tie is perfectly knotted, as perfect as the rest of his outfit. The deputy is impeccable, as always, maybe even more so than Barnes, who appears messy and disheveled at the moment.

I put on a bluff by saying, "Women...go figure..."

"Then why did you get the fine?" Barnes says, chuckling. "But never mind. Tell me, were you in the neighborhood last night?"

I think for a minute. "Yeah, a few meters from Fairbanks, on Burnaby."

"We were hoping you were closer. We would have had a lucky break. So you didn't hear any gunshots, a getaway car or anything?"

I shake my head. "I would tell you if I had. What do we have here?"

Maitland takes me by the arm. "Come on, I will summarize what I have already told the others."

He leads me into another wing, one that, alas, I was very familiar with. I look at the place where I was hiding, on the top runners, behind the rusted silo. From the corner of my eye I see what's left of my clothes on the floor. I must have made a flight of at least ten, maybe fifteen meters. I remember very little, if not that uncomfortable feeling of being traversed by a blade and the taste of blood. Then the flames and ashes.

From behind the carcass of some rusted machinery, a rather strange guy comes out. He looks like he stepped right out of one of those children's films of the eighties or a crime film of the same era. For a moment I can imagine the scene...

"Maitland, where is the stuff you spoke of?" he says, with an American accent. East coast, I would say.

"Over here, Konopski. This is what I was talking about earlier."

Maitland shows him the remains of my clothing. The guy, who

from what I sensed is called Konopski, bends down to look at them. "What's that?"

"Remains of clothing. Burned," says the deputy.

"Great. Something else I don't know?"

Maitland seems embarrassed. "What do you mean?"

"Let it go. This guy here, who is he?" he asks, pointing at me with a thumb.

"Special Agent Harper."

Konopski nods and looks back at the pile of burned clothes. With a pen, he tries moving the pile a little, and then sniffs his fingers. "Harper, huh, what's his role?"

"Pardon?"

The man eyes me and says, "What can you do?"

I give Maitland a questioning look. He responds, "He... he is one of our best detectives. He's smart, I assure you."

"Are you as smart as Chapman or are you smarter?"

Okay, I can tell this Konopski is going to be a pain in the ass, no doubt about it. Maitland says, "Well, that's—"

But I cut him off with, "I'm smarter."

Konopski nods without looking. He continues to sniff his fingers. "Do either of you have a cigarette or something?"

"I will ask Chapman. I quit," says Maitland.

"Well, one point for Chapman then," he says. Maitland shrugs and asks, "Your preference?"

"I prefer something medium or strong, not the ones that are light as air, please. Oh yeah, and even flavored too."

I cannot believe it. Maitland takes the phone, and calls someone to order a pack of cigarettes for Konopski. Who the hell is this guy?

Konopski gets up, goes behind the casing of the machine and comes back with a gym bag. He opens the zipper, extracts a pair of showy white headphones decorated with big black stars and comes back to me. "Harper, I am going to give you my vote of confidence. I need a shoulder, and I was told that you would help me. Now, I want you to make sure that all the time that I have this headset on, no one is to bother me, except when I need a cigarette. Can you do me this favor?"

I nod. "No problem."

"Excellent. Now go ahead and finish discussing the case with Maitland, so I won't have to repeat what has transpired over to you. It is the second time in only a few weeks that I've had to come back here to London, and without notice. I want to get things dealt with expediently, even if I have to go through some pains to fix things. I just want to go home as soon as possible. You understand, don't you?"

I nod again. I try not to feel in awe, but this guy has an overwhelming aura about him, the kind that can make you put up or shut up with no chance to reply.

He puts on the headphones, turns on the music and goes back to take care of the remains of my clothing.

"*I know, something about love...*" He must have it very loud because I can hear the song too.

CHAPTER THREE

"Four bodies, five if you count the pile of burned clothes. No idea of the weapon used, although it's not by fire. There are shell casings everywhere and no one heard a thing. Anything else?" I ask.

Maitland scratches his chin. "The bodies are all naked."

"Yes, naked. But my question is about something else. Who is this Konopski?"

Maitland looks over at him before answering. Konopski is stooped down and singing while he works. Every time he gets up, he does a dance step and then touches a bit here, a little there, as if he's feeling the temperature or texture of the decadent old structure. A dreamer, that's what he is.

"He's a special agent too, Harper. He deals with very specific cases. You remember the Foster case?"

"The rich man with the private museum?"

"Yes, that's him."

"He was the one who retrieved the statue?"

"Exactly. He brought the statue back to us, showed us who killed the guy and even gave us the address to find him."

Nice case. I didn't get a chance to follow the case closely. I was busy with personal matters and wasn't really available at the time. "I understand there were some things you didn't…"

"…Corpses, like these. Naked. This is the third such recent case where we've found a scene like this."

"Three? I must have missed one."

"There was a case awhile back just outside of Brighton. They found three bodies inside an old barn, two men and a woman, all naked. Besides them, in that case, there was another one, fully dressed though."

"Really. Did you identify anyone?"

"A guy named Jerry Cowan. He had some precedent for shoplifting, drug dealing and little things like that. The fact of the matter is it was a criminal neighborhood."

Stanton comes running, with the cigarettes. He hands the pack to

Maitland, nods a quick greeting and leaves.

"Anything else on Cowan?"

"Ah, forget Cowan. They kept our office *loafers* busy for months. We stalked a guy named Clifford Sweetland for a while. He has as a shop selling comics in the East End. The guy's totally batty... got a screw loose somewhere along the way. There's also another one, guy's as big as a closet... they call him Schnitzel, or something like that. A bit of smuggling, counterfeit goods, and nonsense like that. A dead end."

Konopski rips open the pack of cigarettes and brings one to his mouth. "Oh man... a smoke! Maitland, I was asking you for a pack of these, why didn't you bring them to me? I would have preferred Chapman, just so you know."

"Hey, I was the one who ordered them for you!"

"Okay, thank you just the same. I'm done," he says. He lights up the cigarette, takes a breath and closes his eyes. Then he hands me one. "Have one. Don't even think about it. Do you want to take a walk and grab a bite to eat, Harper?"

He didn't wait for my answer, just picks up his bag and leaves. I look for a signal from Maitland who just shakes his head. "After you, Harper. It's your turn this round."

I look, for the last time, at what's left of my clothes. A jacket I had just bought last month, black, that set me back nearly one hundred Sterling, a pair of Italian jeans, a wool sweater at sixty pieces, spandex underwear, and a pair of comfortable boots. All the things I loved. Damn... losing those killed me last night.

CHAPTER FOUR

Konopski wasn't kidding when he said that he was hungry. Sitting at a fish and chips place on the corner, it looks like he has a portion of food for two, as if he had not eaten for months. And he doesn't say one word. Finally when his baskets are empty and he's quaffed a pint of beer, he looks over at me, and winks, satisfied.

"Well, Harper. How was it?"

I blink. "How was what?"

He taps his fingers on the table and smiles at me. "We both know Harper. You took a flight from a great height and ended up catching fire like a match."

I look around, bewildered. "Holy shit, you know!"

"Oh, sorry..."

"But how do you know?"

"I'll be the one asking questions, if you don't mind. What are you, a phoenix? Yes, I think must be a phoenix."

The thing is, when one thinks he's been prudent for years, having calculated all the details, even so far as fooling a police force in London, and in comes a Yankee and with one fucking look he unmasks you.

"You won't tell Central, will you?"

"Why should I? We all have our little secrets."

I take my glass of orange juice and gulp it down. I'm tempted to order a beer, because now, I'm disgraced. I don't think it would make much difference if I get caught with alcohol in my system during working hours.

"Are you going to blackmail me?"

"Quit with the bullshit, Harper. I'm part of an international division that's used to having to deal with people out of the ordinary. You're not so special for me to lose sleep over or that I need to devise a plan to extort whatever money that you may have."

He gets up, takes a few bills from his pocket, throws them on the table, and exits. Already, he has a cigarette in his mouth. Certainly I don't have any idea about his intentions. I guess I'll have to follow him and hope I can figure out what he plans to do with me before I find myself handcuffed in some black van and end up being locked up in a laboratory somewhere in the American desert.

I look around scanning for an exit, an escape from this crazy man. I could run away on our walk back, retrieve the car, and disappear from here. Elbert the printer will help me with a new identity. I'll have to spill to the guy, but at least I'll have a life expectancy longer than I might have as this guy's guinea pig.

And what if I do run? I guess I just can go back to one of my old haunts and disappear from there. Good idea.

I come back to reality when Konopski taps loudly against a glass and shakes his head. He says three small words: *Don't you dare!*

I get up and walk out dejected. I don't know what's so special about this guy, but he's certainly not an ordinary person. I'm afraid he can even read even my thoughts.

"I don't read minds, if it makes you feel any better," he says.

"You just did."

"No I didn't. You just happen to be predictable and I can tell what you're thinking when you have that look."

"What look?"

"The one who wants to run screaming from the big bad Yankee. Now let's move on and not waste any more time. Meanwhile, let's start with us taking a ride in your car, and you can explain to me all that happened in the factory last night."

CHAPTER FIVE

Konopski makes me uncomfortable. I feel my guts tangle up while he whistles to a tune that's only in his head. The more I look at him, the more I realize I don't understand shit about the man. I mean I really have no idea who or what he is.

I drive for half an hour drive and haven't said a word. I try to turn on the stereo to hear something other than his damn whistling, but he turns it right back off, complaining that the music on the radio is no good, and that I don't know good music when I hear it. He's totally bizarre, really. Finally he tells me to turn right on *Brick Lane* and then says, "Right here, stop here in front of that store."

"Which one? I see several stores."

"The comic book store."

"Oh, okay."

The sign reads *Red Devil Comics*, and I think I know who it belongs too. The guy in the werewolf case! Maitland and I discussed the case earlier, and this Konopski guy wants me to meet good old Clifford.

"After we catch up with this guy," he says, "then you can tell me all about what went down last night, okay?"

"Okay. But why are we here?"

"I think that this stop might be of interest to you. Have faith, come on. And if you can refrain from it, don't ask any stupid questions."

I don't reply and make a mental note of his sarcasm.

Konopski goes in before me, the door announcing our entrance with a ringing electronic buzzer. From behind a curtain in the back room, appears a guy with a mustache and glazed-over eyes.

"Good morning," he says.

"Hello," responds Konopski. "I need some information. If you can give us a few minutes of your time?"

The shopkeeper changes his expression, and then smiles. "Please, what can I do for you? You have some questions about comics? Anything in particular you are searching for? Are you a collector?"

Konopski reaches back to the door, turns the key and the opening sign over to say closed.

"Hey," the man protests.

"Calm down, Mr. Sweetland. I'm Special Agent Konopski and this is my colleague, Harper. We don't have any intention of sticking around or anything. We only need a little information."

Sweetland runs a hand over his forehead and then glances toward the back. "Well okay... sure."

"You can tell your friend, Schnitzel, the same things that I just said. No one is going to get hurt here. How about if we go back there and get something to drink?" Konopski looks at his watch. "Some tea, perhaps, given the hour. I wouldn't run from one of your traditional cups this afternoon."

Sweetland leads us to the back room, a large room piled high with stacks of comics, books, boxes, and all sorts of gadgets. At the center of it all, sitting at a table, is is a big man with the look of a dumb ox. I'll bet my ass that it's Schnitzel. In fact, we are introduced and I'm right.

Sweetland sits down and shows us some chairs. He drops like a heap, shoulders collapsing. "What can I do for you?"

Konopski indicates a kettle on a small burner, that's already venting steam. Next, he points to half a chocolate cake sitting on the counter next to it. "We could start with that cup of tea we talked about earlier and a slice of cake. It has a nice look to it. Did you make it, Cliff?"

"No, my sister did."

"Well, then tasting it will be an honor."

Cliff nods, gets up and cuts off a few slices of cake, bringing the teapot and cake over to us. Although I'd rather drink brandy, I have to settle for tea.

"Where do we start? Cliff, first off let me say that we have a mutual friend, and then, perhaps, you will feel comfortable talking to me."

"And who would that be," he asks.

"A tall guy, a bit hairy and threatening, but a good guy, after all."

Cliff scoots his chair back to bump against the wall suddenly and

Schnitzel jumps up, dropping his slice of cake. He promptly collects it, blows it off and then puts a bite in his mouth.

"I don't want nothing to do with him, okay?"

Konopski nods. He takes his slice of cake, smells it, and then takes a bite. He narrows his eyes and rocks his head back and forth with a look of satisfaction on his face. "Hmmmm, Clifford, let me say, this cake is delicious, really."

"Gre... thanks."

"Hey, Harper, you have to try this. I can't remember the last time I've eaten something so good?"

I let myself be persuaded and take a small bite. It's okay... no... it's really good. It's moist, not too sweet. Very balanced.

"Yes, I agree with you."

Cliff has a look of terror on his face, as if he's uncertain whether to flee, to stay, or to commit suicide. Schnitzel bobs his head like a child agreeing with Konopski and blurts out, "You can say that again! This is the best cake in all the East End, really all of London. Don't you agree Chief?"

Cliff has a sudden burst of energy, springs up to slap Schnitzel across his head. "Holy shit, you want me to get rid of me or what?"

"What, Chief?"

"By calling me Chief, idiot."

This Cliff must have a lot of nerve or a lot of money hidden somewhere to manhandle such a brute like that. I recognize the type. He could crush your head with one hand, if he wanted too.

"Calm down gentlemen, here, we are among friends," says Konopski. "Clifford, there's only one thing I need to know."

Sweetland takes one last dark look at his partner and then turns back to Konopski. "What?"

"Where can I find Juan, right now?"

CHAPTER SIX

The suspension of my car starts to cry out when Schnitzel sits beside me. But leaving him behind would have been almost impossible. My CityRover isn't suitable for men of his size. Cliff tries to convince Konopski to let him go.

"Clifford, be reasonable, you've screwed up, and now we have to fix it somehow. Or would you rather Juan give it a try first?"

Cliff shakes his head. "No, it's not my fault, I told you. It's our friend, Jerry, that won't allow me any peace."

"Let's go, Harper. When we get there, we'll talk," ordered Konopski.

I follow his instructions, set the navigator and we all head to the address that Cliff provided. Meanwhile, Schnitzel eats another piece of cake, filling my car mat with crumbs.

"Hey, you want to be a bit neater with that cake, huh?"

"Sorry."

We leave the center of London, moving southward. The fog, so far, has not showed up. The night is clear and cold, so that the windscreen continually mists. Schnitzel falls sound asleep, snoring like a bull in a barn.

The GPS takes me off the main road, towards Brighton and I start to figure out where we are going from here. It's the same village that Maitland told me about this morning, the one where they found the other bodies. After a few miles, I see the outline of the houses and the lights of the windows.

We cross the main road by car, arriving at the bottom, where a church stands. Cliff tells me to park at the rear of the building. There are other vehicles there.

"That priest I was telling you about should be here," says Cliff.

"Fine. Maybe he can arrange a meeting with Juan?"

"Yes, according to Jerry anyway."

Konopski looks in the rearview mirror. He rubs his eyes. Then he claps his hands and announces: "Come on, let's go down."

He knocks on the door of the church. A voice on the other side asks, "Who is it?"

"Good evening, Father, we're friends of Juan." Silence.

"What do you want?" he asks finally.

"Could you please find him and tell him that we have information on the matter of last night?"

We hear some footsteps retreating inside. "Now what?" I ask.

"Now we wait."

"Out here?" asks Schnitzel.

"I saw a pub further back," I say.

"Well then, let's go eat," replied the big man.

Konopski lights a cigarette and looks at the door. He pulls a notebook from his pocket and writes something, rips the page out and slips it under the door. "All right, let's go."

CHAPTER SEVEN

The restaurant is pleasant. It sits in the back of a boisterous a pub in town with a friendly staff and clientele making me relax for a bit. Hell, I almost want to laugh.

I wait for the others to order a drink and I ask for a pint of beer. I'm sure we'll be here for a while. Konopski looks as if he wants to reproach me for my choice of beverage, but he doesn't appear to have anything to say about it.

Cliff and Schnitzel say that they've been here before and that the food's good, if we wanted to order something.

"I'm hungry," adds Schnitzel.

"So order something! Why do I have to tell you everything?" chides Cliff. "I wouldn't want to see your batteries run down."

"Batteries?"

"Leave it."

I am putting down my second pint, when I see Cliff and Schnitzel click like two springs when a customer enters. The man is tall, and dark, and I can't see his eyes. They look like dark holes under his bushy eyebrows. The entire bar seems to quiet down and, after a moment, resumes with everyone talking.

I'll lay a Sterling that the guy who just entered is our man.

He looks around, makes a decision, and in a moment is at our table where he takes a chair and sits down without saying a word of greeting.

"Konopski, you again?" he says in a voice that seems to come from inside a damp cave. I'm not able to discern anything by the tone of his voice. He sounds angry but he doesn't look to be... at least not yet.

"Nice to see you again Juan. But weren't you supposed to be in Italy?" replies Konopski.

Ignoring Konopski, Juan looks over at Clifford and Schnitzel, pointing a finger at them and says, "And you two? Why do I have to cross your path again?"

They stutter, unable to give a coherent answer. Finally Cliff comes out with: "No yellow car this time though."

I decide to break the ice and reach a hand out toward him. "Hi, I'm detective Harper. I say this because it looks like I'm the only one who has not yet had the pleasure of…"

Juan turns to me. I still can't see his eyes. "I killed you last night."

I swallow. "What?"

"I did not know who you were, I considered you a part of the trap and I eliminated you. Only later did I realize two things: one, that you were there by mistake and two, that you are a phoenix. *Post fairy resurgo…*"

I stiffen and slam my fist on the table. "Damn you! Couldn't we have talked about it beforehand?"

My insult doesn't seem to shake Juan in the least. He says, "I wish that I had and also that I did not have to burn those wolves down there too. Even if, in fact, they were disoriented by my surprise."

"Hell man, do you know what I risked?"

"It is none of my business. And if now you are done grieving like a young girl, I would like to know why you tried, although I do have a sneaking suspicion."

Konopski gives a cough, trying to hold back a laugh. "Juan, why don't you talk to these guys first, what do you say?"

"Hey! All I wanted to do is to get close to you, Juan, and I did it," says Cliff, his face turning purple.

Juan shakes his head. "I almost suspect that Konopski has not brought me here just for this."

"If you have finished playing these spy games on old friends, I would remind you of that that, too," I say.

"This is also for you," replies Konopski.

Cliff's guilt becomes evident when he moistens his lips and starts to shake, looking around for help. "Okay, okay… it's Jerry."

"Your dead friend?" asks Juan.

"Yes, him. He can't leave this world and he's pretty pissed off."

"And how do you want to sort this thing out? He died in the barn like a fool. I had recommended for all of you to stay in the circle, but he didn't listen."

"He says that after last night, when you finally extinguished the bloodline of that family of werewolves, he now feels at peace. He just wanted to say—"

Juan suddenly grabs him by the collar and brings Cliff's face a few centimeters from his own. "Say what?"

"He says—"

"No me *Jodas, cabron*! If he's still speaking with you, he did not leave this world."

"Wha ... what?"

Juan pushes him away. "Konopski, we have a problem."

"Yeah, I know. And if *you* say that we've got a problem, it has to really be serious."

Konopski pauses for a moment, then looks at me and he says: "Now it's your turn to tell us how you ended up in that factory last night."

CHAPTER EIGHT

"I'll make it short, or at least I'll try to. I'm a phoenix, but I think we all understand this by now. I don't know when or how it happened. I don't know if I was born this way or what. I did some research, talked to some people, often with charlatans, but nobody has been able to explain it to me.

"I died for the first time when I was a little less than twenty years old. I was biking, I hit a tree and bam, I woke up a little later in the same spot, stark naked in the middle of a pile of ashes. I was covered with soot from head to foot. The bike, of course was burnt to hell, as well as my clothes.

"I wiped the ash off as best I could and covered myself with what was left of my leather jacket. I crossed the miles that separated me from my house on foot, shivering in the cold.

"For some years nothing happened, until I joined the police force. And then I found myself murdered in an alley from someone who, obviously, did not like that I had intervened in their criminal activity. And guess where I woke up? In the place where I crashed the bike, just like the first time.

"It took several attempts before I realized that every time I died I was continually waking up where my first ashes lay. I assure you that death is not pleasant in any form gentlemen, far from it. When one has such a *gift* we certainly shouldn't take it lightly. But, sometimes, to be honest, I can be kind of reckless.

"After a few years I built a shelter where I placed my first resurrection ashes, in an effort to not to get discovered by my colleagues, friends, and the woman I love. One problem remains, however: the fire. You see when I die I burn up like a wicker man. Just like that movie with Christopher Lee.

"But back to last night, I was there because someone had informed me that I would find news about what I am. It may seem strange, but I want to be normal and not risk ending up in some dark laboratory being dissected by mad scientists. You surely can understand this, right?

"Well, my informant calls me and gives me this tip. There would be an exchange between some people of a certain object; he wasn't able to tell me exactly what, and that if I showed up I would get all the information I was looking for. He had found this out through his channels, and by observing a strange man in the East End. And now, I think we know who this strange man is."

Konopski applauds. "Bravo. So you then thought you'd sneak in and try to intervene in this exchange between gentlemen. How did you plan to take away this item? You'd lose your badge if they'd arrested you."

"My plan was to observe, more or less," I admit.

"Let me see if I understand," Cliff intervenes. "Am *I* the weird guy? And someone informed on me?"

"Yes," we all respond in unison.

"Okay, okay, I just wanted to know."

Where did I go wrong, I wonder. I feel like a child in elementary school… the child in special education class. Luckily, I have Cliff and Schnitzel to save me from the first and second place.

Juan removes something from his bag, a dark skin tube. Removing the cap, he pulls out a sheet of papyrus. He lays it on the table. At its center, the page is blank. On the sides, like a frame, are a series of red symbols and some red splotches.

"Is that blood?" I ask.

"Yes, of course it is. It's what was often used in creating spells and incantations."

"Oh," I say.

Konopski approaches for a better look but he does not touch the sheet; he only observes it closely. He doesn't even smell it like he does all of his other examinations.

"Who is it supposed to be?"

"*Halphas*, from what I understand."

A silence falls over our table, so that I get the impression that the entire room is silent with us. I hear a loud ringing in my ears and my vision blurs. Then everything returns to normal, when Konopski nods and says, "Well, you're right, we're in deep shit."

95

"Yes, we are." says Juan.

"So what happened?"

Juan binds his long hair back in a ponytail, revealing a pair of golden earrings. He reminds me of a gypsy.

"Someone, perhaps a witch doctor or some sort of insane cult priest, gave this sheet to the family of werewolves and it came into Jamaine's possession. And I fell for it. They drew me there to give me the tube as sort of peace treaty between us. At least that was what he promised. Once I got there, I had to take out some of their hidden sentries on the runways, including this sucker," and he eyes me, "and then I went down to get the tube. When I took them all out, I realized that the tube was empty and that the paper was in the pocket of one of the men I had killed."

Konopski whistles. "Nice play. And so Halphas figured it out as well. How did he get away?"

Juan shakes his head. "There was no one alive to stop him, at least not in there. He must have escaped, and who knows where."

The situation gets heavy for everyone. It's hard for me to believe what I am hearing; it sort of put my own problems into a better perspective.

"You're telling me that something that was blown away in the factory last night is now going to come back to haunt a Londoner?"

"Not a something, Harper, a demon who was imprisoned in that paper," explains Konopski.

"I think I'll order another pint, if you don't mind," I say.

CHAPTER NINE

Tony the cap jumps on one foot, once, twice, three times, like a naughty child and points a finger at me. "You asshole! Bringing them here... these... these..."

"...Gentlemen," I finish the sentence for him. "We want to know who is playing the tip that you gave me."

Tony the cap, earned his nickname not because he wears hats, but because of an old story about bottles of counterfeit wine and how he became agitated over a debutante at a dance where he was drunk on his ass and stoned out of his mind.

"Look, Harper, this is going to screw up my business man, you know?"

Konopski walks forward and gives it to him. "Listen, are we going to get down to business or not? Officer Harper has dealt with you much kinder than I would have, now you need to politely answer his question."

Tony whines and looks around desperately. "But you guys are cops!"

"Yeah, Tony. Now tell me something new," says Konopski. "Like how, we forget about you and your *business.* Deal?" He stretches out his little finger to seal the deal. Hell, he's almost more disturbing than Juan.

"All right," replies Tony. "But get the big guy out of here first."

Konopski and I turn at the same time to look Schnitzel. "Him?" I ask.

"No, no, the other big guy. The one who's built like a bodybuilder..."

Juan makes a gesture with his hand and walks away a few steps, finds a chair, sits down and picks up a book at random from a table.

"Okay, there's this guy in the City, one with enough grain to keep half of London. He sent me this henchman one day asking me to find him a quiet place for a meeting."

Konopski puts a hand on his shoulder. "Slow down a minute. How do you know a guy like that," he says, pointing around the room. We're not really in the kind of place where would you take a girl on the first night, or maybe even the second."

"Wine. Harper knows. I deal in rare Italian wines and I was able to procure a extremely rare bottle for this person."

"Procure. I like the term. I guess it's all handled with the necessary trappings, right?"

Tony smiles. "More or less."

"Go on, that's better."

"So, this guy called Amédée, puts up a sheaf of Sterling... that's enough to last me for two years. I just have to find him this place. I try to gain some information from the henchman, you know, to protect myself a bit and to get a better understanding what kind of transition will be made."

Juan sighs. "Yes, I understand *your particular kind* of ethics."

"Hey man, there are things I do not want to deal with, believe it or not, dude."

"It has been years since I've heard the expression *dude*," says Juan. Then he goes back to reading his magazine.

"Well, in the end, the guy tells me about an exchange of *endothermic* material and so I start asking a few more questions, pouring him a drink to loosen his tongue. This tells me that it must be something genius and worthy for me to—"

This time I have to stop him. "Endo what?"

"*Etrotecnico.*"

"I don't think what you just said is a real word. Maybe *esoteric*?"

Tony nods. "Whatever. At that point, what was I to think? My friend Harper, here who has long asked me to be his eye if anything comes my way like that. So I called you, Harper, with the tip. Hell I thought I was being a pal!"

I light up a cigarette and start spinning my wheels, trying to stay ahead of my associates. I can see that Juan and Konopsk are both deep in thought, as Clifford and Schnitzel are sitting like two dogs on a chain, like they were caught stealing good meat from the pantry. I can't think of who may have sold the sheet to Amédée starting this whole mess.

"Who sold the sheet to Amédée...?" I ask no one in particular.

"Hard to say," Juan responds first. "I myself am looking for the other pages, since this my business, so along the way I have created a few enemies. Amédée is among them. More than once he has used this ploy to try to lead me into a trap. This time it seems that, for better or for worse, he succeeded."

I turn to Juan. Before speaking I light up a cigarette and take a couple of deep hits to relax. "Amédée. You knew him before?"

"His family has long been trying to kill me. An old feud came out of a simple misunderstanding, if I can call it that."

"Who or what are the members of this family?"

"An old French lineage. Werewolves."

Clifford snaps suddenly erect, stands up and makes a run for the exit. Juan stretches out a leg to land him sprawling among the shelves. "Cliff, what's wrong?" he says.

"Juan, Juan, the wolves! I don't want to die!"

"Chief, tell him," intervenes Schnitzel.

Juan gets up, takes Clifford by the collar, lifting him up and drags him over to Schnitzel. "What do you have to tell me, Schnitzel?"

Clifford continues to fuss, trying to break free from Juan's tight grip.

"Jerry. The man, who handled the deal, said there is a contact out on you. Jerry told me so."

Konopski, Juan, and I look at one another, and I realize that we just took a step backward in solving this thing.

CHAPTER TEN

Clifford hangs up the phone and spreads his arms. "Why did I have to call him?"

"Don't expect much. After all you know him," says Konopski. "Now we have to decide what to do. Do you have any effective spells, Juan?"

"Bring him to me, keep busy and I will resolve it."

"What?" I ask. "Should we be here too?"

Juan turns slowly towards me, giving me a chill. "Cliff and Schnitzel are the only ones out of the game now. You two do your part. Are you afraid of dying, phoenix?"

Cliff and his brutish partner snap to attention and move a step closer to the exit. Konopski blocks the door before them, though. "We didn't say that you could leave yet."

"Why not?" asks Cliff, "what are we still needed for?"

Konopski taps him on the forehead. "You're staying with us, jerk. We need to understand how involved your friend Jerry is with this story. So, when the carrying demon comes back here we're going to have a long talk with him."

"This is all we needed," complains Cliff.

"Harper, call the center and ask for a couple of men to come here, to keep an eye on our new friends here. I wouldn't want them to slip away."

So I'm reduced to acting as a delivery boy for this capricious Yankee, his gloomy friend, a mischievous ghost, and a couple of two-bit criminals. I can't find an adjective to dare even to them, would be fun. To avoid upsetting Juan, I call the center and ask for reinforcements.

"They'll send two men as soon as possible. You two need to be aware that you are in their custody, and that they have the right and duty to use the Taser if they need to. Got it? Especially you, big guy, you understand?"

Schnitzel nods. Cliff does too.

Konopski looks at his watch. "If you need to drink, eat, pee, smoke or something else, do it now, because when we are there with our friend, it's going to be a lot of fun."

"You especially will need to expect some surprises. He will not be alone," says Juan. "He will bring someone along with him, knowing him as I do."

I crack my knuckles. "Well, what's the problem?"

Juan sighs. "We're not going to a fistfight, Harper. Have you ever seen an escaped demon, one that has been imprisoned for hundreds, no, thousands of years in a sheet paper? I do not think it will be willing to fall on its knees after a punch to the jaw or a couple of shots to the stomach."

My arms fall to my sides and my shoulders slump a little. I begin to see more clearly what Juan has just described to me. I even feel a shiver go down my back, sort of like how I feel when I die. My true abilities could be put to the test in front of a supernatural being? I can presume to burn one last time, before anyone has figured out how to give me a normal life.

"What should I do? I don't have any special powers, other than what you already know about."

Konopski lights a cigarette and says, "You can take care of Halphas. One shot… one kill. I hope you are a good shot, boy."

I take my gun from the holster and check it over trying to gain a little confidence. Something tells me that, in this case, a gun won't be appropriate for the situation.

CHAPTER ELEVEN

Hiding behind a column, I feel as nervous as the first day of school. I'm pretty sure I look that way too. Juan and Konopski are in the center of the room, an old pub undergoing renovation. They seem less concerned with me. Konopski has brought those funny headphones, and keeps them stuck around his neck, like a DJ who expects to start working soon.

At eleven o'clock, the doors open. Four men and a woman enter the building. A woman? I wouldn't ever have expected that. And she's the one giving the orders, I can tell right away.

The other four seem to be ordinary people, perhaps people recruited at the last second as Juan speculated. Cannon fodder, sacrificial victims to distract my teammates as she attempts to eliminate Juan and take what he has from him.

"Juan, is a pleasure to see you," she says. " It seems our meeting has been postponed for far too long."

Juan does not move. "Halphas, get to the point."

"Right. Did you bring what I asked you?" She glances at Konopski, as if to weigh him, looks at him with disdain, and then back to Juan.

"I have to disappoint you Halphas. You asked things of me that I cannot give you. On the other hand, if you were so kind as to return what came from inside the page, we can keep seeing each other as I had planned."

The woman steps back, turns to the door and then began to laugh, surprising me. They are stunned, even the four suckers at the door. Suddenly she stops laughing and orders: "Take out that guy."

The four unsheathe cutting weapons, rather long and oversized. I think that they're some type of machete, or something. Without waiting to find out what they are, I focus on the closest one, making him do a pirouette on himself.

I see that Konopski has slipped headphones on now... and then suddenly he's gone. I continue to fire until I see him appear behind the back of one of the three survivors. The man falls to the ground, for no apparent reason.

"Hey Harper, why don't you be careful with that fucking gun? You want to put a hole through me?" he screams.

"But where...?" Where the fuck did you pop up from?"

The other two are thrown behind the tables, trying to take shelter. They seem less eager to use their knives. Juan instead, is still leaning against the counter with his arms crossed. Blessed is he who manages to stay so calm at a time like that.

"Let go of the knives, you two!" he says in a low growl. The guys, in response, get up and try to take Konopski, who barely touches them with some kind of whirlwind movement, causing them both to collapse.

"Hey, didn't you hear my friend?" he says. "Harper, check to make sure there aren't any more ready to come in."

The woman, Halphas, does not seem to be flustered. I look past her without blinking. I open the door carefully. The street is deserted. In this neighborhood, all business is over for the day and they don't seem to care about gunshots I just fired off.

"All quiet," I say.

Juan stretches, Konopski walks around the woman. They look like two predators waiting for each other's next move. I don't see, however, any noticeable concern in the woman.

After an interminable silence, I hear desperate cries, a clanging of armor and battle cries. The sounds appear to come from the woman who from nothing produces a dull black blade. Where the heck did it come from though?

She attacks Juan, but he pulls out a weapon very similar to her own. Konopski beckons me to move back and to take no action. As if I had any intention?

"Shut your ears," cries Konopski, running to me. I follow his advice, trying to drown out the cacophony of sound that hits us.

The woman's agile, but Juan seems to be the wind. And it is the wind that begins to rage inside the pub, making the lighter objects in the room fly. Then he turns into sudden flames that start to burn everything in the room like fuel. I feel sorry for the owner of the pub. I hope it's insured.

Everything seems to last for a long time, between thrusts, parries and dodges. They move like dancers, but dancers more angry and ferocious than I've ever seen. Until a sweeping slash from Juan stops the dancing. Clean and precise, the severed head of the blond woman, rolls across the floor.

Konopski jumps up, reappearing behind the counter, with Juan's skin tube. "Here," he cries.

The man pulls out the sheet and begins to chant something, which gradually turns into a series of sounds, rather than words. And I lose consciousness.

CHAPTER TWELVE

A light tapping on my cheeks wakes me up. I open my eyes and find myself, with difficulty, having smoke blown into my face by Konopski. At least I'm sure that I'm not dead this time. I'm in my car, fortunately, lying on the back seat.

"Well, partner. Now we must prepare for the deposition to be released over to Barnes and Maitland," he says. "Get your ass up."

"Give me respite, please. What should we write in this report? Some chick that housed a demon, came up against a bad guy, tall and dark, and that they fenced with black swords?"

"More or less. Don't worry, I have everything ready for you to read, learn your part and then sign."

I scratch my head and get out of the car. I need a drink. The only pub close by is burning down. "And Juan?"

"Who knows? He's took off, vanished, as he always does."

I'm looking for a pack of cigarettes in my pocket. The package is crushed. I pull one out anyway, straighten it, and light it up. "Listen, can we go have a drink?"

"Sure. I need to get something to eat too. After all that exercise, I need carbs."

We go to a pub on Rupert Street, a quiet place that closes late and accepts orders even after midnight. Konopski orders fish and chips once again along with a pint of beer. I take a sandwich and a dark beer. In the room, besides us, there are at most ten people.

"Okay, this is bullshit but I'll sign it, but nobody would believe the truth, let me tell you."

"Bravo Harper. I can tell you, however, that these documents will go out of our hands to those of Barnes where they'll end up in a drawer even before I'm on a plane headed back home."

I bite into the sandwich, reflecting on what he's telling me. Basically I believe him. He shows up out of nowhere, has me waiting on him like a bloody porter, there's fire and flames, people talking to ghosts, a demon in the body of a woman and he knows that if I die I burn and I am reborn in the ashes. Why would not I believe him?

"All right Konopski, I trust you."

"Harper, I hope I never have to investigate you," he says, and he does so quite seriously.

"Me?"

"No one, besides the two of us, knows what you are in Central. Don't you be taking any more shots to the head like in the factory."

"Konopski, mind your own business."

"I hope you're not one of those one day."

We take a long time, before we finish eating and drinking and leave the pub. I give him a ride back to the hotel without speaking.

When he gets out of the car, he gives me a nod, and then he goes into his room without looking back. I don't feel comfortable, knowing that there are people around like him and Juan. From now on I'll be looking over my shoulders, more than usual.

While I'm driving home, a song comes in my head, the same one Konopski sang when I met him at the factory. How did it go? I turn on the radio trying to dismiss it... and suddenly I find myself there, as if someone had sent me.

"I know something about love. You've gotta want it bad If that guy's got into your blood..." I start to sing.

THE END

The songs mentioned
- The Marcellus - Blue Moon
- John Denver - Leaving On A Jet Plane
- The Zombies - She's Not There
- The Zombies - Tell Her No
- The Exciters - Tell Him

Born in Mirandola, Italy in 1976, Marco Siena was an early reader cutting his teeth on such diverse authors as Franklin W. Dixon, Edgar Allan Poe, and H.P. Lovecraft.

The rudiments of writing were learned from an exceptional teacher at the Italian Technical Institute who instilled in young Marco the passion for Gothic romance and terror that he already loved, but also taught him the structure and elements essential for this kind of fiction writing.

Marco spent almost twenty years writing RPGs where he learned technical discipline and gained experience in the refinement of a personal style. But only with the advent of the Internet did he get to see his own stories become published in various anthologies. His next step was to participate in a small publishing house competition that he won hands down. From that competition came his first novel, *The Nine Stars*, published for that imprint. Two years later a second novel, *Before Vanish*, was also published.

Marco's first self-publication was *DD1: Ignition*, a novel that begins a steampunk/horror trilogy that has met with favorable reception among fans of the genre. From there, he hasn't slowed down, continually trying to refine the minimalist technique of authors he admires like Raymond Carver, Elmore Leonard, and Joe Lansdale with whom he feels a writer's bond.

Currently, Marco writes in different formats, from short

stories to novels. The second installment of the steampunk/horror trilogy *DD2: Combustion* is in the works and he's finishing a paranormal noir expected out in 2016. His favorite genres are noir, horror and thriller, all served with strong doses of irony.

Raven's Head Press

Brings you some cool gothic horror

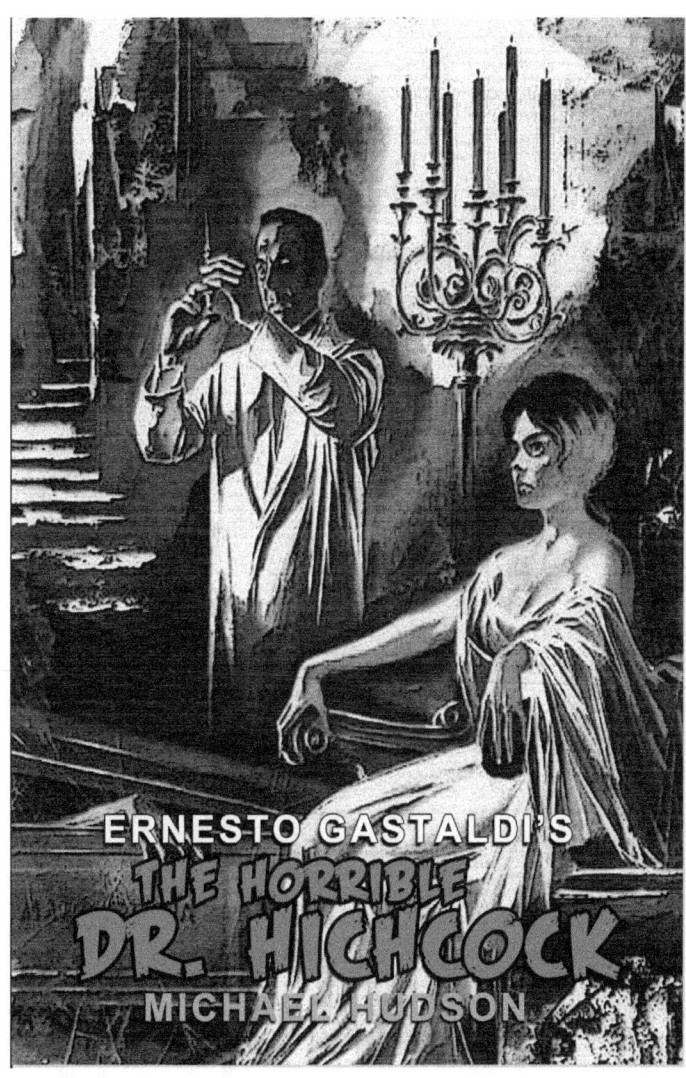

www.ingramcontent.com/pod-product-compliance
Lightning Source LLC
Chambersburg PA
CBHW060131260626
47160CB00005B/2072